With an international reputation [...]
Ron Butlin is also one of Scotland's leading poets. At various times he has been a lyricist with a pop band, a footman, a male model and a barnacle scraper on Thames barges. He now lives in Edinburgh with his wife, the writer Regi Claire, and their dog.

His works include *Night Visits* and *The Sound of My Voice*, and a collection of themed short stories, *Vivaldi and the Number 3*, all published by Serpent's Tail, as well as four books of poetry and several radio plays. Most recently, the French translation of *The Sound of My Voice* was awarded the prestigious Prix Mille Pages 2004 and Prix Lucioles 2005 (both for Best Foreign Novel).

Praise for earlier titles by Ron Butlin

The Sound of My Voice

'One of the greatest pieces of fiction to come out of Britain in the '80s... Butlin's book is a stylistic triumph... I anticipate that *The Sound of My Voice* will receive the recognition it deserves as a major novel' Irvine Welsh

'One of the most inventive and daring novels ever to have come out of Scotland. Ron Butlin is that rarest of breeds – a poet who takes the novel form and shows that it is ripe for reinvention. Playful, haunting and moving, this is writing of the highest quality' Ian Rankin

Night Visits

insight and reassuring compassion about people who have exhausted their own supplies of hope, yet in his hands they are never entirely hopeless' *Time Out*

'Beautifully structured ... Butlin empathises as well as any writer dealing with the pain of adolescent trauma I've read... What makes the achievement special, however, is the way in which warped adolescent yearning is interwoven with a very different and repressed yearning, that of Malcolm's Aunt Fiona [who is] an archetype of inner corrosion and suffering... Butlin handles the delicate savagery of her condition with a rare combination of sympathy and detachment, and its climax... is as fine in its portrayal of psychological destruction and reconstruction as *The Sound of My Voice*' *Books in Scotland*

'Sick, disturbing, menacing, exceptionally good... Excellently depicted and a credit to the skill and compassion of Butlin, this is contemporary fiction at its classic best' *The Void*

'Butlin's crisp prose oscillates between the real and the surreal, providing the perfect poetic metaphor for this powerful portrait of corrosion and pain' *Glasgow Herald*

'In his dark debut novel, *The Sound of My Voice*, Butlin pulled the reader into a world of twisted longing and inner fantasies among fractured characters. This second novel reaches for the same depths and, as with the best psychological tales, succeeds because it leaves the real terrors to the imagination' *The Scotsman*

'This Bergman-bleak novel is devastating but eventually uplifting. Marvellous' *Uncut*

'Though the setting lends itself to gothic overstatement, Butlin's exploration of emotional abuse is shocking without being sensationalist. As Fiona draws the boy away from his mother into her fantasy world, he is careful never to let repugnance for her as perpetrator outweigh sympathy for her as victim' *Guardian*

Vivaldi and the Number 3

'This collection is an extraordinary read. It is extraordinary in its concept, extraordinary in its delivery, extraordinary in the emotions it manages to evoke... wry, satirical and deeply moving... heart-stoppingly beautiful... [Butlin] is a master' *The New Review*

'Brilliantly conceived... Playing with biography (though never fast and loose) Butlin nips seamlessly in and out of anachronisms, conflating history like a squeezed piano accordion... [he] can take an idea and fly with it to the far reaches of his imagination, developing oblique studies not only of the composers themselves but of their music' *The Herald*

'These stories are hymns to the artistic temperament' *The Times*

'Wickedly funny... witty and contemporary' *Classic FM Magazine*

'Richly surreal stories... an unalloyed triumph... light and yet learned. Gloriously anachronistic... playful, funny and accessible. Wit, humanity and daring ... A brilliant and surreal collection of sketches' *Sunday Herald*

'Funny, eloquent, quirky and desperately sad... Everything is mingled in Butlin's world – past and present, dream and waking – with daring and deftness ... (A) bubble of lightness (that) somehow carries up with it a heavy stone of sorrow' *Independent on Sunday* (Five Star Review)

'A deft balance between the comic and the moving... there's a passionate humanity in the stories ... compelling... powerful... expressed with a breathtaking clarity and precision... full of hard truth, darkness and light' *The Sandstone Review*

Other works by Ron Butlin

Fiction

The Tilting Room
The Sound of My Voice
Night Visits
Vivaldi and the Number 3
Coming on Strong

Poetry

The Wonnerfuu Warld o John Milton
Stretto
Creatures Tamed by Cruelty
The Exquisite Instrument
Ragtime in Unfamiliar Bars
Histories of Desire
Without a Backward Glance: New and Selected Poems

Drama

The Music Box
We've Been Had
Blending In

Opera libretti

Markheim
Dark Kingdom
Faraway Pictures
Good Angel, Bad Angel

Belonging

Ron Butlin

A complete catalogue record for this book can
be obtained from the British Library on request

The right of Ron Butlin to be identified as the author
of this work has been asserted by him in accordance with
the Copyright, Designs and Patents Act 1988

Copyright © 2006 by Ron Butlin

Published in 2006 by Serpent's Tail,
4 Blackstock Mews, London N4 2BT
website: www.serpentstail.com

Designed and typeset by Sue Lamble

Printed by Mackays of Chatham, plc

ISBN 1-85242-915-1
ISBN 978-1-85242-915-7

10 9 8 7 6 5 4 3 2 1

This novel is for Anthony, Béatrice and Malcolm, Catherine and Lyell, Donald and Kath, Dora and Lucas, Graham, Louis, Luise, Marie and Roger, Nigel, Randall, Pam, Tom and, of course, my wife Regi – with sincerest gratitude to each of them for helping me to belong.

Special thanks to my agent Malcolm Imrie, and to all the team at Serpent's Tail.

Acknowledgements

Early drafts of two short sections of this novel first appeared in *NeonLit – The Time Out Book of New Writing* (editor, Nick Royle) and in *The Third Alternative*.

The author would like to thank the Scottish Arts Council for a Writer's Bursary which allowed him time to complete this book.

March 2003

1

From the slopes of Mont Blanc across the valley, a glacier-edged wind set the ski chairs swinging like hanged men. The screech of metal on metal came echoing back from the walls of the four luxury apartment blocks.

Company of a kind.

The sky had darkened too early; the clouds were swollen and sagged down almost to within touching distance – more snow was coming our way. So let it, I thought to myself.

Drifts already lay heaped around the private resort of Les Montagnes Blanches, covering everything in one upward sweep rising to the ski slopes and mountain ridges above, and spreading down to the village of St-Ciers some five hundred metres below. The paths I'd just cleared would soon be covered again. Between low banks of shovelled snow, they led from the main door of our apartment block to the oil store, the parking area and the garbage dump. Darkness was falling rapidly.

Standing at the edge of the almost empty car park, I was enjoying a close-of-day glance down into the valley when I heard a car approach. I looked round – to meet the glare of its headlights full on, then watched as it pulled into a parking space under one of the security lights. A Ferrari, wet-look red, with Paris plates. The driver cut the engine and got out. Tall, rich and tanned; he didn't even bother to glance in my direction when turning to zap-lock the doors. Seen just from the back, the girl seemed a good bit younger: chestnut hair streaked blue, orange and green, long leather coat and Doc Martens. Sexy looking too.

Firework hair and Gucci luggage – that was my first sight of Thérèse.

With an age difference like that, they had to be father and daughter – but then I saw the man put his arm round her in a most unfatherly way.

Husband and wife? No chance.

Flakes of fresh snow began to drift down as I watched Monsieur Ferrari swipe-card his entrance, then stride through the glass doors into the apartment block opposite, taking his something-for-the-weekend along with him. Not that I was envious.

Not really.

I was more pissed off at being taken for granted, like the rest of the scenery – the snow, ice, jagged mountains and the Alpine cold tightening its grip. At two thousand metres it gripped to the bone. Not even a word of thanks for the stretch of parking I'd kept scraped clear on the off-chance one of the apartment owners might arrive. Maybe M. Ferrari assumed it didn't snow on his space.

Anna would have heard the car arriving. She'd be waiting for me.

But first I had to check that there was enough fuel for the

emergency generator. Once inside our apartment block, I went down the basement steps and unlocked the cellar door. On with the light, a rub at the glass and I read the fuel gauge. Nearly full. Even if a blizzard did cut us off we'd survive, no problem. In fact, being left to ourselves was the best thing for both of us, Anna especially. When I came back up, the snow was already falling thick and fast. Through the glass doors I allowed myself another close-of-day glance down into the valley. For several moments I stood and watched the lights of St-Ciers coming on one by one. Abruptly, a whole tangle of brightness appeared: streetlamps, presumably. From here, the village looked like so much smashed glass.

Yes, the good life was over.

Then I entered the skis-boots-and-outdoor-clothes room. It was larger than my mother's flat back in Edinburgh and came complete with brass hooks, lockers, benches and tiled flooring – everything done in hardwood, not a splinter of cheapo pine in sight. Anna was bound to be getting frantic by now – and so, with methodical slowness, I removed and hung up the *gardien* cap, unbuttoned the *gardien* jacket, took it off and placed it in my locker. Having carefully unlaced each winter boot in turn, I wiped them dry before placing them neatly, side by side, on their special mat. I took several minutes to lace up the indoor trainers. I needed time to get my story straight.

Anna was in the sitting room, pretending to read.

She looked up. 'Well, so what are they like?'

'Didn't really see them. I was in the basement checking on the generator, just in case.'

'The first people here in a fortnight, Jack – and you didn't even look?'

'Bad timing. Probably already indoors by the time I'd locked up. They wouldn't hang about in that temperature. Really cold out there now.'

Danger safely past, I began getting into my stride. 'Wind's just starting up, and snow. Looks like we're in for some heavy weather.'

'Their car?'

'Ferrari. This year's, and blood-red.' Then I heard myself add: '*Gucci* luggage.'

That one small phrase, and it was all over. I couldn't believe I'd said it.

Anna put down her book. 'I thought you didn't see them?'

'Didn't *talk* to them, I said.' One small slip – that was all it took.

'Man? Woman? A couple?'

I shrugged. No matter what I said now, she'd assume I'd been hiding something. Which, it seemed, I always was.

2

At thirty-two, Anna was the older by three years. She had fair hair, blue eyes and her body was slight and always restless. Flirtatious, funny and quick, she was attractive both to men and to women. She was a nursery-school nurse, and a very good one. She was caring. A bit too caring, as I had gradually come to learn.

We had met the previous summer, back in Edinburgh – and on our first date, a few romantic beers in the bar of the Café Royal, she told me that she'd been an accident. While she talked, my eye was suddenly caught by the words 'Wedding Party' appearing as a screen caption on the television that was fixed high on the corner wall behind her. What a good luck omen, I thought.

'An accident?'

So she explained: unwanted. She'd been the tail end of the 1960s peace-and-love fest gone very wrong. Having arrived in a taxi, her mother had simply walked out of the maternity hospital the following day, and kept walking. False name and address, of course. Not that Anna herself could remember anything; the full story was a threat frequently used by her foster parents – set number one, that was. They hadn't wanted her so much as the social security support money that came with her. Same for set number two. Anna laughed, 'I hated them – and I was great at tantrums!' By the time she was placed with set number three she'd been classified as 'a hard case'.

The television screen was now showing the wrecked remains of a restaurant. Even though the sound was turned down, I could make out that the wedding had been in Afghanistan and had been accidentally bombed by the Americans. Then President Bush came on, mouthing like a fish in a glass tank, and a few seconds later the picture cut to a dim, greenish glow, like an underwater scene, crisscrossed by strands of brilliant light – a night attack on Kabul.

Anna was still talking: 'But they softened me up, let's say. It was third time lucky – I left home at sixteen, but still keep in touch with them, just.' Her working with children had been inevitable, she pointed out: she needed to lavish on them the tenderness she herself had longed for as a child.

I was impressed. Anna seemed to know a lot about herself.

Very quickly she seemed to know a lot about me too. According to her, a loving relationship was something to be *worked* at. She was a woman who gave everything of herself, and expected everything in return. Until I met Anna, I didn't know what love was – or pain.

A couple of months or so after we'd started going out together she turned up early one September morning at the Comiston Road flat where I was grouting the new tiles in someone's bathroom. She'd brought an advert:

URGENT: RELIABLE COUPLE WANTED. HANDYMAN and HOUSEKEEPER to act as caretakers for luxury apartment complex in French Alps. Accommodation provided.

'Well, Mr FixIt, how about it? I've phoned them already. Seems they've been let down and are desperate. We fax them our CVs and if everything's fine we're to get there in time for the weekend rush.'

By lunchtime it was goodbye to her nursery school and goodbye to the tiles and the grouting. I was deliriously happy. I was in love. We EasyJetted over on the Wednesday – the first anniversary of 9/11, the only day on which there were spare seats, nearly a planeload – unpacked on Thursday and started on Friday.

After our fast-track romance, the first month at Les Montagnes Blanches was a kind of easeful honeymoon. We were a world away from the cobbled streets of Edinburgh, from Saturday shopping among the hordes on Princes Street, from Bush's War on Terror – though, when watching CNN, we'd catch him strutting about, and later on we'd see him telling Hans Blix and his team to look harder for weapons of mass destruction – to us it all seemed very unreal. My *gardien* duties done for the day, I'd shed the cap and overalls to take Anna's hand for long romantic walks along the mountain paths, followed by candlelit dinners that came with a view of snow-clad Mont Blanc opposite. Our evening would be rounded off with starlit sex in bed, our king-size, caretaker bed. Not that we were ever alone – between the king-size sheets, especially.

'Love me, love my analyst' was written in blood on the bedroom ceiling. Back in Edinburgh the Big A had been Anna's saviour and mentor three evenings a week. Spiritually speaking, he'd EasyJetted over with her to become our chaperon-cum-chauffeur on our journey together along life's analytical highway. I'd make a casual remark, a casual gesture – and we'd stall. Out she'd get and take the moment apart as per the Big A handbook, tracing every tone and nuance back to its childhood source to discover what was wrong. Problem located, she'd launch into some gestalt-gabble, explaining to me what I was *really* feeling or *really* meaning. Problem fixed, we'd climb back in and our journey through life would continue.

Until the next time.

Therapeutic pit-stops like these were dotted round the very circular track that had become our life together. Yes, she was perhaps a bit too caring. By the following March, the Big A was our daily companion and the blood on the bedroom ceiling was well and truly mine.

For the two weeks before M. Ferrari's arrival, the private ski resort of Les Montagnes Blanches had been all ours. When the *pistes* were bad the owners stayed away – handing over their luxury apartments to the care and attention of housekeeper Anna and *gardien* me. Thanks to our passkeys, during that winter we had inspected every apartment in every block. Sometimes one quick glance in the door was enough; at other times we'd stay the night. Twenty-eight flats in total, including the penthouses. We lived the good life: liberating a Bordeaux here and some bubbly there, sampling from freezer-fuls of smoked salmon, lobster and caviar, partying in the private Jacuzzis and saunas. When the skies were clear, we got padded up like moonmen and went scrunching across the unmarked snow and ice, our footprints freezing into position behind us.

Even though I honestly believed I didn't fancy the girl with firework-coloured hair who had just arrived, according to Anna I probably did – *subconsciously*. That was always her trump card: she knew my subconscious much better than I did. Much, much better.

That night I woke up at four-fifteen by the bedside clock and found myself alone. I got up and went through to the sitting room. Anna was standing at the picture window, staring out at the other apartment blocks and the near-empty car park. Darkness, the falling snow, the security lights, the snow-covered Ferrari, our snow-covered VW rustbox... there was nothing else. The faint screech from the ski chairs, the wind whining in the steel cables – that was all she had to put between herself and the pain she seemed unable to live without.

Just like when, having caught me out over Thérèse's arrival that afternoon, she had immediately started firing from the hip: *A couple?/Is there a woman?/What's she like?*

Not even pausing to reload before: *How old is she?/Did she speak to you?* Merciless – that sting in her voice, that pain in her face, and each question a whip-cut that no answer of mine could heal. It was unbearable to watch. She became frantic about small details that meant nothing:

What was the woman wearing?

I hadn't noticed.

Why not?

It wasn't important.

So what was more important that you did notice? She tore and tore at herself to get to that nothing. When she'd failed to uncover what had never been there in the first place, she had burst into tears, said what a terrible woman she was, so jealous, so cruel – and had started whipping herself all over again. Anna honed everything, even love, into a weapon to turn against herself.

It was snowing steadily. A good moment to cross the room, to take her in my arms and soothe her, reassure her. A good moment to comfort her. Instead, I stood and watched while what seemed an eternity of weightless flakes settled in silence on the far side of the glass. Anna was unhappy and, beyond giving her a comforting pat, I had no idea what to do about it.

When she returned to bed nearly half an hour later, I pretended to have just woken up.

'We should get married, don't you think?' she whispered.

Not knowing what to say, I pretended to go back to sleep.

3

It was still snowing the following morning.

First thing after breakfast I went down to the basement, the electricity nerve-centre for the whole complex, to run through the checklist of *gardien* precautions in case the power failed. With one flick of a switch I took all the lifts out of the circuit. Mr Efficiency – until, a moment later, it occurred to me that I should have made sure that none of the lifts was actually in use just then. Well, if anyone was trapped I'd soon hear about it – there were emergency phones.

Next, as the apartment lights had been flickering on and off every so often, I needed to give the back-up generator a test-drive. It was a split-new generator, which meant split-new problems, but at first press the green button marked START fired it into action without a single cough or spit. The red button marked STOP stopped it instantly.

Before returning to our flat, I went outside, crossed the car park and stood for a moment looking down towards St-Ciers. The village had vanished and so had most of the valley – a curtain of dingy greyness was swirling towards us, shutting out everything as it came closer. The clouds were curdled to a dirty yellow – a storm was approaching, rapidly.

Just then I had a terrible thought: when I'd neutralised the lifts, had I also cut off the emergency phones?

Too late now.

As I came in, Anna had the radio blasting out. The invasion of Iraq was a few days old and the announcer was saying something about suicide bombers. I turned it down.

'I'm going across to ask them if they need anything.'

She looked up from where she was kneeling on the floor brushing her outdoor boots. 'They're on holiday, Jack. They'll want to be by themselves.'

'It's my job to see that everything works and that the clients are provided for, especially with a storm coming.' I allowed her a reassuring smile. 'Back in a few minutes.'

I turned to go. She reached up and laid her hand on my arm.

'It's their first morning. They're probably still in bed. If they need anything, they'll phone down.'

Sometimes at moments like this I had no pity. I didn't want to hurt her, but whenever I was given the chance I couldn't seem to help myself. Getting a bit of my own back was always the excuse – assertion therapy, Scottish-style. That jealousy of hers gave me a little power now and again.

I was about to put my arms round her when the phone rang. Shit! Somebody must have been in a lift – and I'd trapped them. I let my hands drop back to my sides. The phone had to be answered. That's what I was being paid for, after all.

In my best *gardien* French: '*Allo. Les Montagnes Blanches. C'est Jack McCall, le gardien, qui parle.*'

It was the girl. Evidently, when M. Ferrari engaged them for the weekend he expected them to play at secretaries as well, even for distress calls.

I started straight on the defensive, getting in quick about the lifts and the emergency phones. I should have saved my breath, and my French. She replied in English: 'The lift? Not the lift. The lift is not the problem.'

'Yes?'

Then her English broke down. She seemed quite agitated. Something about the heating, it sounded like. I was to come now. *Now*, she repeated. A nice voice too, with a kind of nervous, sexy tremble to it.

I told her I'd be there in a few minutes, then hung up.

'Their heating's on the blink. Probably just the radiators needing bleeding.'

I waited for Anna to say something. She didn't move but simply stared out of the window at the snowflakes being jerked from side to side as if the air was receiving electric shocks every few seconds. She didn't look at me, and she didn't speak.

I had the *gardien* cap, the boiler suit and the bag of tools. Mr FixIt was ready to leave.

I left.

4

The storm had really arrived: an ice-honed wind came howling and gouging along the valley, and snow was tumbling down in heavy, sullen lumps. I stood in the doorway and gathered my strength for the trek across the open car park to the neighbouring building. Even with my hand up to shield my eyes, I could hardly see twenty metres in front of me. It was more like looking at the lightly scribbled marks of someone's unfinished sketch: the apartment blocks, the Ferrari and our VW rustbox pencilled in faintly. Above me the cable and ski lift had been so badly drawn as to be more like the remains of a tattered web.

No sky, no mountains, no road, no valley – nothing but falling snow. If it continued like this, we would soon be cut off.

Shoulders hunched into the wind, I battled my way like a hero to the rescue, across the car park wasteland and through the swirling snow to M. Ferrari's block. The main hall was warmer, but only just. I kicked the snow from my boots. Probably M. Ferrari hadn't set the thermostat correctly. Caretaker problems always came down to the same thing: the helplessness of the rich. The wind was hurling itself round the building, and from nearby came a desperate keening lament. The small ground-floor reception had been closed up a month ago, but someone had left a window open. I slid the panel shut, snibbed it, and the keening abruptly stopped. The hall at once felt sealed in and secure. Outside, the landscape was almost completely blotted from sight, as if there was no world any more and the sky a threat still to be carried out.

Up the first staircase, and I could hear another sighing voice that became more heart-rending with every step. By the time I reached the top floor I felt an icy blast: the penthouse door was wide open and through it came what seemed like a dozen voices wailing and raging as one. I stepped inside, pulling the door behind me. Anna and I had once checked out the flat for its fun potential and decided to pass: too minimalist for our taste. Bare walls, designer space and most of the furniture made from glass and steel tubing – chic and bleak. The place would probably feel chilly even with the heating full on.

The rainbow-haired girl was standing in the near emptiness of the main room, hugging herself round the waist. It was sub-zero, yet she was wearing only a thin blue dress.

For a few moments neither of us spoke. The room was in

chaos: a full-scale blizzard was gusting in through a balcony door that was mostly a large hole ringed by jagged glass. The wind clawed at the curtains, sending them billowing up into the air; it howled its way round the room and back out again. The polished flooring was a swirling carpet of snow, the white flakes whirling up in my face, the cold stinging my skin. A bamboo table lay on its side, and what might once have been a vase had smashed to a dozen pieces on the floor.

The girl addressed me in English: 'Out there.'

'Pardon?'

'He is out there.' She pointed towards the balcony.

So what? If the Paris prat wanted to freeze, that was his own business. The room was a fucking disaster area – 'trouble with the heating' was an understatement.

'What happened to the glass door?'

No response.

'I'm the janitor, *le gardien*. You rang down about the heating.'

'The heating?'

Was she on drugs or what? I tried again:

'The glass door, *mademoiselle*? What happened?'

No reply. She looked in a bad way.

One last try: 'Look, where's your husband?'

'No, not my husband. No. He's out there. Please. You go and look.'

I went and looked.

When I came back into the room, she was standing over by the glass-topped dining table.

'He is dead? No?' She was keeping herself upright by

gripping the back of one of the chairs.

Was she going to faint there and then? She'd started shivering and looked very pale. Twenty years old, at most.

Trying my best to sound sympathetic and professional at the same time, I nodded gravely: 'I am very sorry, *mademoiselle.*'

There was no reply. The wind was still raging, the snow still hurtling round the room. She wasn't even looking in my direction but was staring down at the floor, her hands gripping and re-gripping the curved steel of the chair-back.

I tried again, a little louder to be heard above the wind, and more gravely: '*Mademoiselle*, I am very sorry.'

That worked. She fainted.

I watched her legs buckle, her hands lose their grip... and she fell. There one minute and gone the next, like she'd been unplugged at source. She lay in a huddle on the floor, her hair a rainbow spread over a patch of drifting snow.

Almost immediately, though, she started coming to. She was mumbling to herself, then, without any help from me, she sat up. 'True? He is dead?'

I nodded again and put my hand on her shoulders.

She looked up into my face. 'And now?'

The man lying out there was old enough to be her father, and a bit more besides. Old enough to be *my* father, almost. For a split second I had the terrible fear that if I glanced towards the balcony it would actually *be* my father's body I'd see lying out there. I took several steps towards the balcony door... and abruptly was once more looking at the body of a complete stranger. M. Ferrari-Penthouse. This was his flat: a disaster of wind and snow, curtains wrenched and flapping, broken glass everywhere, and a girl I'd never met before, crouched at my feet and asking me what was going to happen next.

I moved into masterful mode and, without answering her, strode across the room to a designer grotto of mirror, glass and steel beading that I was certain would be the drinks cabinet. I poured a large brandy, put it into her hands and told her to drink it up.

She did.

'Better?'

'Really dead?'

Yes, and lying at full-stretch out on the balcony. Shouldn't he be brought inside? Touching him didn't seem right... yet I couldn't just leave his body sprawled like that in the snow.

Suddenly the girl screamed. She screamed again. And again. Three loud screams, then she stopped. There was a moment's silence, as if the storm had unexpectedly stilled. Then once more the wind came battering in through the smashed balcony door. She got to her feet. Her whole body was shaking with cold.

'You believe?' Her face was pale. Her hands balled into tight fists, she shouted: 'Please, please. You believe me?'

I took a step backwards. 'Believe you? I don't understand— '

'Snow for the champagne, he said. Champagne in the fridge. It is still there. I show you the bottle.' She was almost yelling to make herself heard above the storm.

'Champagne? It doesn't matter about the bottle of— '

'Then he slips, he grabs for me and— '

'Take it easy. Don't— '

Already she's dragging me towards the balcony door and pointing outside.

'You see? There he falls. Just there. On the snow. Much

ice under the snow. He turns and... and he hits into the window...'

Now she's stepped over the body and is out on the balcony. I follow her. She bends down and starts scraping away the snow.

'You see? You see?' She pulls me down next to her. The wind's battering at us from every side. She's shouting in my ear to make herself heard. 'He slip on ice, I say. He turn and— ' She points to another spot a couple of feet away; she's raving on and on '— maybe *there*. You check. You can speak for me.'

'What is it I'm looking for?'

'You will tell them? You will say you believe me?' She starts screaming again – 'You believe me. Please. Please' – as she kicks at the drifting snow. She dashes back indoors.

I look down at the snow. I look at the broken glass door. I look at the dead man. Now what?

I was stepping back into the flat when she returned from one of the side rooms carrying a bundle of clothes: a fluorescent orange and blue ski suit, a red dress, stockings, something in green velvet. An ivory-coloured silk scarf was trailing from her arm.

'He bought all things for me to wear when we are here.' She hurried over to the broken balcony door and threw everything on to the dead man, then rushed off again. Seconds later she returned with more. 'Many things. He loved me. Yes. Yes. He loved me. And I wanted to tell him. I wanted to say – everything. To tell everything.' She dropped the clothes, fell on to her hands and knees on the snow-covered tiles. The snow continued to fall, and the wind was catching at her hair. All at once she leaned forward as if exhausted and buried her face in the heap of brightly coloured material on the man's chest.

Then she began to weep.

I stood to one side and looked on. What the hell was I to do? What was I expected to do?

I watched her begin tearing at the clothes, ripping them to pieces. Then she started beating her fists into the heap of torn clothes and burying her face in the tangled mess she'd strewn across the dead man. All the while, she was screaming and weeping.

I pulled her back, intending to bring her out of the storm and into the flat, where I'd hold her until she calmed down. Then I'd ask her name, I'd ask who the man was, I'd ask where they'd come from. These things established, I'd proceed to secure an explanation of what had actually happened. That was the plan.

Instead, she went limp in my arms. Ice-cold with snow clinging to her hair and shoulders. Quite exhausted.

'Leave me alone. Please.' Again she began to cry. I held her while she wiped the snow and tears from her face and sobbed brokenly over and over: 'Leave me alone, *monsieur*. Alone.'

Abruptly, she shook herself free and got to her feet. She repeated in a firm voice: 'Leave me alone!'

Next thing, she'd rushed back into the room and straight out the door. She was running down the stairs, yelling: 'LEAVE ME ALONE! LEAVE ME ALONE!'

A leather coat hung over the back of the couch. I grabbed it and hurried after her, taking the stairs three at a go. By the time I reached the reception hall she'd vanished into the storm.

For several moments I stood staring through the glass front door at the elemental chaos outside. I could hardly make out the other apartment blocks looming all but invisibly nearby. The block opposite, where Anna and I lived, was totally hidden by driving snow. I peered into the endless white.

'ALLO! *Mademoiselle!*' I shouted. Then, in the midst of the swirling whiteness, I glimpsed a flash of blue. I dashed in that direction and – of course – her footprints! That was all I had to do: follow her footprints!

Into the driving blizzard, calling out every few metres, the human St Bernard was lumbering to the rescue.

I was soon gaining on her; I saw her stumble and fall. She didn't get up. I could hear her sobbing.

She was on her knees when I reached her, clawing at the snow and at the ground underneath. She was shrieking and screaming. Her blue dress was sodden through, her hair hung wetly, she'd lost her shoes and the soles of her feet showed through the rips in her tights. She was smearing snow and dirt over her face.

I crouched down beside her.

She ignored me and continued digging her fingers into the drift. I could see earth on her hands; her fingers were bloody, her skin raw with cold.

I put my hand on her shoulder.

She didn't notice. I draped the leather coat over her.

'*Mademoiselle? Mademoiselle?*'

Suddenly aware of me, she turned round, stared for a moment in silence. Then, with unexpected dignity, she lifted the wet hair back from her face. 'Thank you, *monsieur.*'

5

Having brought her into our flat – where Anna at once moved into maternal mode and took Thérèse, as the girl called herself, off to get cleaned up and comforted – I struggled back once more across the car park through the raging snow. As I made my way upstairs, I could hear the wind roaring unchecked above. When I'd rushed out I'd left the apartment door wide open. Now, as I reached the top of the stairs, it seemed like a hurricane was coming towards me, almost knocking me off my feet.

Once inside the flat I closed the door. Things eased slightly, but the snowstorm continued tearing in through the smashed patio window, to go rampaging full-blast round the penthouse, setting the floor-length curtains waving wildly right up to the ceiling, blowing loose papers and snow in all directions. The room was freezing cold; my breath came in icy clouds.

Out on the balcony, the dead man, whom I'd learned was a M. Bertrand, had amassed a respectable covering of snow for such a short time.

Now what?

I was only the caretaker, I reminded myself. Not the undertaker. Cleaning things, mending things and being nice to millionaires – OK. But no one had said anything about dead men when I applied for the job. There'd been no mention of distraught girlfriends/mistresses either. Was there a Mme Bertrand somewhere, and did she *know*? Would I have to phone her? Should I call a doctor? The police? An ambulance? Was the road up from St-Ciers still passable?

Beside the receiver lay a Les Montagnes Blanches courtesy handbook listing all the numbers the owners needed to know, including that of the head office in Paris.

I dialled for an outside line.

It was dead. I phoned down to Anna to ask her to try. It was still dead. I tried the mobile – CALL FAILED. And again – CALL FAILED.

That was that, then. Les Montagnes Blanches was cut off.

Back out on the balcony, M. Bertrand was looking more like a snowdrift by the second. Clearly, he couldn't be left here. Something had to be done. I took a deep breath and bent forward into position. A firm grip with both hands. Then I pulled, and kept pulling.

He was heavier than he looked. His head lolled in the snow; I had to cradle it against my arms. The heel of his right shoe snagged on to the base of the doorframe; I had to free it.

Once I'd dragged him inside and slid shut what was left of the balcony door, I pulled the curtains, then used a matching set of four red cast-iron cooking pots from the kitchen to secure them in place, hoping to keep out the worst of the storm. I was about to leave when I had a last-minute thought. After a search through the hall cupboard I found a spare blanket – this I laid over the dead man. Then, having turned the heating right down, I left, locking the door behind me.

For nearly a full minute I stood at the top of the stairs waiting for my heart-rate to return to normal, my hands to stop trembling.

In no time at all I was back. When I'd given Anna a progress report, she'd stared at me in disbelief. 'You didn't leave the poor man just lying on the floor, did you?'

'I couldn't lift him.'

'The two of us can.'

So Anna and I returned. Once heaved on to the plate-glass dining table, the late M. Bertrand seemed to be hovering in mid-air – as if a magician, having passed hoops round him to demonstrate the success of a new trick, had lost interest and simply walked away, leaving the dead man floating in nothingness. The blanket covering made him look more 'at rest', but only just.

The day before my father died, he'd been brought home and laid on our front-room table because the bed was too soft for his broken back. He'd been a roofer.

I looked down at M. Bertrand and shivered.

Enough was enough, I thought. I'd come back and tidy the place later.

We were just leaving the flat when Anna suggested that as the phones were down I should try getting to St-Ciers to inform the authorities; I could also contact Paris from the village. Why didn't I ski there? she suggested.

For once, common sense took over. 'Ski – in this weather? I'd soon need to be rescued myself.'

'The rustbox?'

Driving our ancient VW came strictly under the heading of hard work any day of the week, and as for coaxing it down the hairpins to St-Ciers during a snowstorm... My look must have said it all.

'Well, in that case— ' Anna pointed to a set of keys on the hall table, '— you'd better take the Ferrari.'

6

Into the bodyform leather racing seat. Belt on. Ignition on. The dashboard a space console of red, blue and green pulses. Snowflakes hurtling towards me in their thousands. Ferrari man. *Vroom-vroom-vroom...*

A minute later I was ever, ever so slowly first-gearing my way across the car park, the snow scraping the low bodywork. The wipers, set at hyperspeed, kept the windscreen more or less clear, but it was like driving through a meteor storm with the meteors coming thicker and faster.

Assuming I reached St-Ciers, would I be able to return?

Second gear. Out of the car park, the road like a white-walled corridor with metre-high snowbanks on either side. A gentle press on the accelerator...

The car gave a roar and surged forward.

A minute later, having skidded into a drift, I climbed out. The Ferrari's boot and rear window were completely buried. Looking down to the first bend, I could see that the snow was piled more than twice as high. The car was stuck. I was stuck. We were all of us stuck.

Back in from the storm, the hero was greeted by Mother Anna announcing that Thérèse was now tucked up and would soon be fast asleep. We were by ourselves again: two Good Samaritans old enough to know good deeds never go unpunished. And the punishment was about to begin.

23

7

We knew that once the road was open the place would probably be overrun. There'd be police, an ambulance, maybe even a helicopter. This was our last chance to party.

While Anna prepared the necessaries, I returned to the basement to redirect the heating and switch the emergency generator into standby mode, ready to kick in the moment the electricity failed.

When I got back she was scribbling a card. 'No need to tell her where we're going,' she said. 'We'll just leave a note.' She propped it against the coffee pot:

Dear Thérèse,
We'll be back later. Hope you had a good sleep.
Help yourself to whatever you fancy.
Love, Anna

Like two naughty children sneaking out of the house, we closed the apartment door with the very silentest click, then hurried upstairs two steps at a time – Anna carrying the picnic basket, me with a bottle of wine in each hand.

Outside, beyond the stair windows' triple-glazing, the snow looked like it would continue erasing more and more of planet earth for a good while to come. Where we were going we wouldn't miss it.

Thanks to my Mr FixIt trickery with the heating circuit, the apartment we let ourselves into was warming up nicely, better even than snuggling back into bed. No chic and bleak minimalism here, but cosy French-Scottish baronial. The owner, a M. Dubois, didn't stint himself – and neither would we. Thick red pile up to our knees, an elephant's foot for brollies, antler head for the coats, scarves and hats, a line of portraits and landscapes on the walls, each with its own brass light. Music? A centre panel of buttons, dials and pulsing red lights set in the hall gave us what we wanted, when and where we wanted it.

Well, we wanted music – and we wanted it *now*. No having to suffer in Trappist silence until we'd struggled through to some unit in the far-off living room. There were speakers landscaped into every wall, a panel in every room and zappers never far from reach – and so, lifting the nearest from a hall table of solid granite, I zapped us whatever we might have left in the player from our previous visit.

One of the classics. Mick Jagger at his best.

Anna kicks off her shoes, does a bump and grind down the corridor, stripping off T-shirt, skirt and underwear as she goes. I follow.

Leaving our clothes where they fall, we Adam-and-Eve ourselves to our most favourite picnic spot in the whole of the French Alps: the luxury *en suite* bathroom *chez* Dubois. The curtains drawn across the small window, the shaving light tilted for discreet ambience, our perfumed picnic candle flickering gently on the marble-topped cabinet. Seconds later, we're up to our chins in a swirl of warm, foamy water.

Unpack the picnic basket. Drinks first: a Bollinger courtesy of the Dubois' cellar and a Crozes-Hermitage from their neighbour, a banker with Crédit Lyonnais who'd also been our unsuspecting host on several occasions during the winter. For snacking: some thawed-out Ardennes pâté, smoked salmon, caviar, strawberries, a choice of salami and *jambon cru* and *baguette*. Everything microwave fresh. The freezers were likely to pack in due to the need to conserve electricity, so this was by way of salvage, a modest attempt to cut waste.

'Cheers!' We raised our glasses to M. and Mme Dubois.

Waving my brimming bubbly in a circle wide enough to take in the rest of the world, I called out: 'Absent friends!'

And that's when I remembered the late M. Bertrand.

From her sudden silence, so too did Anna.

We drank.

I poured us another. The wine bubbled over, some spilling into the Jacuzzi, some on to the floor tiles.

'Careful, Jack. Don't waste it.'

'The caretaker peasant can lick it up later. A chance for him to moisten his daily crust!'

There was a love-seat ledge running round the inside of the Jacuzzi. I leaned over, making the water level fall between Anna's breasts, and topped up our glasses. The sight of the love of my life, in all her nakedness and beauty, stretched out so invitingly within reach was having its customary effect – which she noticed, and took hold of.

Having playfully dipped my prick into her glass, she licked off the drops of champagne. She glanced up. 'The cocktail swizzle-stick?'

Some water splashed over on to the floor tiles. I joked: 'More work for that caretaking peasant! Must do our best to keep him in a job. Don't want him starving to— '

Another silence. This one lasted much longer.

Finally I put down my glass. 'Look, Anna, we did all we

could for M. Bertrand. We're sorry it happened. We never knew him. We can't get in touch with anyone. Once the phones are working again, we can get things sorted. We're sorry, but what else can we...?'

'I suppose so.' She took a sip from her glass. 'Anyway, I'm glad Thérèse is asleep now. Poor thing was worn to nothing.'

Anna was letting herself float completely on the surface while the water bubbled round her. I began stroking the inside of her leg.

'Poor Thérèse,' she murmured.

I was hardly listening. Open the red first, to give it a chance to breathe while we made love? Or else just keep going with the caresses until it was time to move straight into action? Anna was saying something.

'Pardon?'

'Imagine, I said, if Thérèse was a few years younger. She could be our daughter, near enough.'

Our daughter? That stopped me.

I could see that Anna was getting more relaxed. At her best, she was the most relaxed and lascivious woman I had ever met.

But – our daughter?

I started the caresses again almost at once, hoping she'd not noticed: stroking, smoothing, sliding my hand up and down. I swirled myself round into position between her legs.

Anna was still talking: '... and if we'd a boy, you could show him how things work and how to mend them. You'd like that.'

I swirled closer. Time to move things forward; once she got started on about kids, there was no telling what she might do, or not do. Like forget to take her pill. It would be her subconscious forgetting, of course, not her.

She smiled. 'I was actually jealous at first, can you believe it?'

Again I stopped stroking. Then started almost immediately. And kept going. She kept talking.

'Imagine being jealous of broken toasters and leaking taps! I'm a wiser woman now. Sometimes I smash a cup on purpose – did you know? – just to see the look of pleasure on your face as you concentrate on fitting the pieces together. Yes— ' she stroked the side of my face with the empty champagne glass, 'you'd make a wonderful father. Of course, if we'd a girl, then I could— '

My fingers, already hard at work, moved into overdrive: it was *Anna* I wanted. Of course it was. No one else – certainly not that rainbow-haired teenage waif, not after seeing her in her grief and distress. I leaned forward to kiss the love of my life and stop her talking. Meanwhile, no hands! I'd slip it straight in, and that would be that.

'Keep going, my caretaking man, keep going.' She opened her legs a little wider. 'Mmm...'

'Our daughter!' I heard myself half-laughing.

At once, Anna put her palm against my chest, pushing me back.

'You don't want to have children, do you?'

'My greatest want, at this precise moment, Anna – '

'I'm being serious, Jack.'

'So am I.'

She jerked herself back down on to the love seat and glared at me. 'You're so fucking selfish sometimes.' Then more gently: 'We've done the living-abroad-and-having-a-good-time bit. It's been fun. Time to move on. Why don't we get married, have kids and be happy? Everybody else does.'

'We're happy already, aren't we?'

'Are we? Are we really, Jack? Being stuck in a fucking snowdrift until our contract runs out and we're told to leave? Is that happiness?'

'It was *your* idea to come here, remember! I thought you liked it here.'

'I do, but not for ever. And it's for ever I'm thinking about now. Not just the next couple of months. I want us to have a home, a real home of our own – not someone else's, nice though it is.' She waved the glass to take in the hand-painted tiles, the gilt-edged mirrors, the fluffy towels, then managed a quick smile.

'Don't look so scared.' She patted me on the arm. 'Mummy'll look after you.'

The Jacuzzi foam continued bubbling away between us and 'Angie' came from somewhere hidden in the walls. A slick of misted grease had formed over the salmon, the caviar pot stood in an oily-looking puddle. In my sincerest tone of voice I said: 'You know I love you.'

'I believe you.' She wasn't smiling. 'When men say "I love you" they usually mean "I need you". But I believe you, God help me.'

'Angie' finished. During the silence between tracks I said: 'I really do, Anna.' I gave her my sincerest look. After all, I meant what I was saying. Every word of it. I took her hand and for several seconds I felt very close to her. Then I let go.

'Shall I open the red now?' I reached for the bottle and the corkscrew.

I went through the labours of peeling back the foil, pushing in the corkscrew, turning it and pulling firmly. The cork slid out with a satisfying pop.

'Do you want a clean glass or— ?'

She gave a sniff and wiped her eyes. 'The fucking wine, Jack? Is that all you can think about? The fucking wine, you – you shit!'

All at once, and with the worst timing possible, Mick was cut off in mid-'Cloud', and the discreet lighting gave out. The Jacuzzi's swirling slowed down and stopped. The room, apart from the light from the picnic candle, was in darkness. So much for the split-new generator.

'What a fucking place!' she cried out, slamming her hand flat down on the suddenly slack water. 'What a FUCKING, FUCKING place!' She hit the water again and again. All round us, the shadows cast by the picnic candle leaped back in alarm.

'Anna!' I tried to grab hold of her hand. 'Anna!'

'Get yourself the fuck out of here. Find what's got broken down and fix it.'

'But Anna— '

'Don't touch me!' Still crying, she twisted herself out of my grip. 'Go and fix the fucking thing – that's what you're paid for, isn't it? It's your job, so it's your bloody fault!'

'My fault? The new generator's hardly been used. There are always teething problems— '

'Your job's to keep it running properly, and it's not running properly.' She got to her feet, sending the water sloshing over the sides. 'So it's your fault. You're bloody useless.'

'A minute ago you were saying— '

'*Caretaker!* What a joke – you can't even take care of yourself.' She clambered out of the Jacuzzi. 'Yes, it was my idea to come here. But we came here together, remember. I gave up everything to be here – and where are we?' Turning to face me, she aimed a glare at me, right between the eyes: 'Well?'

Well nothing. Any answer would be the wrong answer.

'OK, fuckbrain, I'll tell you where we are.' She picked up one of our host's thick towels, wrapped it round herself and screamed at me: 'Halfway up a fucking mountain and in the pitch fucking dark, thanks to you. You... you fuckbrain! FUCKBRAIN! FUCKBRAIN! FUCKBRAIN!' In time to her cries, she stomped round the bathroom and kicked the champagne over to send the empty bottle clattering across the tiles. Her hair was wet and straggled on to her shoulders, and her face was running with tears, soapy water and Jacuzzi foam.

'Anna, stop behaving like— '

'Don't you tell me how to *anything*! Just fuck off and get that fucking generator fixed!'

I stood up but, torn between wanting to placate her and wanting to get the hell out of there, I hesitated – and remained in the Jacuzzi for a moment too long.

'You still here?' she shouted, her face anger-blotched. 'Then the fucking picnic's all yours!' She picked up the red wine and poured the entire bottle into the water, drenching me. The salmon followed, then came a shower of caviar, salami and strawberries. Lastly, the perfumed candle burned an arc in my direction, missed me, hissed into the water and went out.

A moment later, having blundered about in the dark until she found the door, she stormed off.

I suppose some men would have gone after her, would have reasoned with her, shouted at her, put her over their knees – hoping that from then on she'd be nice as pie. Such a show of strength might have made her feel secure.

Maybe.

As I stood there, up to my knees in rapidly chilling water that was littered with pieces of sodden bread, and with a slimy trail of caviar and mixed *hors d'oeuvres* running down my chest, I thought about acting the macho man. And thought long enough to have second thoughts.

8

Having got myself dressed in the near darkness and felt my way down to the basement, I mended the emergency generator. Nothing to it, in fact – the manufacturer had installed the wrong strength of fuse. Then I returned to clean up the bathroom, now discreetly lit again.

The place was already quite chilly, dripping wet and a complete mess. I did my best to collect together all the food debris and dumped it, together with the bottles and glasses (none broken, thank goodness), into the picnic basket. I washed out the Jacuzzi, then used a few fluffy towels to mop the floor reasonably dry.

It took me a good twenty minutes. Job done, I went across and stood by the window. With the glass wiped clear, I watched the snowstorm raging outside. At least the view looked good: an Alpine scene of snow, wind-torn fir trees and the hint of mountain peaks seen through a blizzard that looked even more impressive than I'd imagined before leaving Edinburgh.

Without warning, fingertips had come to rest on my

shoulders. I hadn't heard her coming back in. I knew exactly what was going to happen next.

She was going to say she was very sorry.

She was going to say she needed me.

She was going to say she loved me.

It was a familiar pattern that could be summed up in the familiar equation: total contrition + total forgiveness = ecstatic reconciliation (probably on the tiled floor).

It would be a glorious, incandescent, mind-expanding, post-craziness fuck... and afterwards we'd promise each other the world all over again. Letting ourselves be wounded and healed – we called this *love*. And, for those brief moments, it probably was.

Craziness, then forgiveness. More craziness, then more forgiveness. That was love. That was us.

Without turning round to face her, I moved my hands behind me to let them rest on her waist. She was wearing one of her lightweight dresses. I could feel the warmth of her body under the satin-soft material. I pulled her up against me.

Then turned to kiss her – and at once took an abrupt step back, straight into the radiator beneath the window.

'Christ, Thérèse! I thought you were Anna.'

A split-second's pause, then she replied:

'I called out, but you did not hear.' She didn't look angry, but then she didn't look pleased either. In a very subdued voice, she added that Anna had made afternoon tea for the three of us.

'Listen, Thérèse. I'm sorry for...' I left the sentence unfinished.

'Things happen.'

'It was a genuine mistake.'

She shrugged. 'Mistakes happen.'

Having picked up the sodden towels and the picnic basket of empty bottles and trampled *hors d'oeuvres*, I found myself repeating what my old piano teacher used to say at the end of every lesson: 'That's enough for today, then, eh?'

We went downstairs.

For the second night in a row I woke up. Someone was crying in the next room. Stifled, choked-back sobs.

Between the sobs I could hear an unbroken murmuring. Not the precise words being said, only the rise and fall of two voices running into one. Thérèse's voice: hesitant, halting and unsure; Anna's: always sympathetic, always reassuring.

I slipped on my dressing gown and went through. Thérèse was sitting on the couch crying, and Anna was holding her, smoothing her hair, stroking her. I paused in the doorway. Thérèse continued sobbing and whispering in half-French, half-English while Anna listened. Without make-up and playing 'daughter' to Anna's 'mother', she looked even younger.

A blanket had been placed round Thérèse's shoulders. When I was turning to go I saw it begin to slip.

Back in bed I waited. When Anna returned, I took her in my arms. But as we made love I couldn't help picturing the rainbow-haired waif from the storm and her borrowed off-the-shoulder nightdress.

9

Over breakfast, between sound swoops and static on the radio, we learned that the Iraq War was taking its course. Baghdad was being hit on all sides and wouldn't be holding out for much longer; meanwhile, British marines were pushing towards Basra. Another suicide bomber had blown himself up. Of more immediate concern to us, however, was the bad weather – it was expected to last a few days. We were completely cut off and would be staying cut off for another day at least. Until then, I would have to conserve energy and check on the emergency generator every few hours. We were well prepared: enough food, enough water, plenty of candles. No problem, really. Except for the presence of the late M. Bertrand.

The side door of our apartment block had to be forced open very gradually in case the wood cracked or the metal hinges snapped clean at such a low temperature. Easing it back a centimetre at a time, I found a second door, of drift-snow, shutting us in.

No problem for Mr FixIt. Putting down my bag of tools, I shovelled almost a metre clear, then began to dig a rough path through the blizzard.

Well over an hour later I reached the apartment block opposite.

Once upstairs I went into the penthouse suite, opening the door carefully to avoid letting in a sudden rush of air through the smashed balcony window. The room was icy, but now there was a semblance of peace, thanks to the line of cooking pots weighing down the curtains. Though the wind still shrilled and tugged at the thick velvet, they remained closed – and only light flurries of snowflakes swirled round the room. First things first: clear up the mess and make a better repair job of the window. I righted the bamboo table, swept up the smashed porcelain. The carpet was littered with unmelted snow and broken glass; it was difficult to tell between them.

The blanket had stiffened in the intense cold. Having lifted it, I saw that M. Bertrand was exactly as he had been left, except for the occasional small icicle. Maybe he had become frozen to the table? We hadn't thought to lay anything underneath. When the time came to lift him, would he need thawing out?

All at once a rush of wind ripped into the room, knocking me to one side. Behind me, the curtains tore themselves free, sending shadows racing across the walls; more snow gusted in. I looked across the room and *there*, in the doorway, stood Thérèse, staring in amazement at the uproar she was causing.

Over the howl of the wind I shouted to her: 'Close the door! You have to— '

'*Pardon*.' When she let go the handle, the door slammed shut. The whole room shook.

'*Pardon*... Sorry.' Then she moved towards the table. 'I will be with him a little.'

Thanks to having been dressed by Anna in some of her own, less flamboyant outdoor clothes, Thérèse now looked like a normal teenage girl: neatly brushed hair, sensible winter jacket, sensible winter shoes.

'I understand, Thérèse. I'll leave you. I can come back later.'

'Don't go. Not necessary to go. I will sit with him. That is all.' She knelt down at the table edge, her hands clasped in front of her as if in prayer. She was holding back her tears. I turned away to get on with my work.

Once I'd measured up the window and fixed the curtains in place again, I went down to the ground-floor reception to find something to use as temporary boarding. Ten minutes later, after hunting round in the cellar, I came across an old picnic table. I hammered and chiselled at the top until it came off. Because the lifts were out of action, I had to haul it all the way upstairs. When I returned to the penthouse, I found Thérèse still kneeling exactly as before, and still sobbing quietly. She didn't look up.

With the temporary screen mounted, the room was quieter and darker. Not an exact fit, but all round the edge there was a halo-brightness and thin slashes of glare between the slats that made the room seem a bit like a church or a chapel of rest. A good job well done. Now to check on the rest of the flat. I tiptoed discreetly away into the next room.

After six months of Anna's perpetual 'socks to be kept in the drawer clearly marked *Socks*', the master-bedroom was my kind of tidiness. The downie lay thrown across the bed as if someone had just climbed out; crumpled black-satin sheets; pillows scattered haphazardly, some of them lying on the floor. A white underskirt hung on the back of a chair. The silk was very cold, like frost that wouldn't melt even when touched. How could I possibly have fantasised about the poor girl while making love to Anna the previous night? The dressing-table mirror was clouded over. An abrupt movement in the glass: Thérèse had come into the room.

I watched in the mirror while she stood for a moment to collect herself. Not a glance at the tumbled bed. She wiped her cheeks. Then, having reached towards her underskirt, she seemed to change her mind and instead came over to me. There was something bright and glittering in her hand; she held it out to me.

'My necklace. It is broken.'

'What?'

'My necklace. Here. Please. Silver, real silver. It breaks when... when he... when he falls... You understand? It gets broken.'

Was she meaning that her necklace got broken because M. Bertrand had reached for her as he slipped and grabbed hold of it? At a time like this was she really wondering about the state of her jewellery? A bit cold-blooded, or was it what Anna would call 'displacement activity'? Should I try asking in French? But probably things would get even more mixed up. The girl was just upset. Very upset.

'You're French, aren't you?' I asked.

She didn't look up, but was trying to hold the ends of the broken chain together as if the silver might join itself. 'Yes, French – but also I live in Spain. I am there some time. I'm back living in France now.'

'So where are your parents?'

'*Maman*, she still live in Spain.'

'And your father?'

She looked up at me. 'Anna say your job is you fix things. You fix this, please? Real silver.' She held out the broken chain. There was a crescent moon pendant attached. 'You can glue?'

'I will try to solder it – like glue, for metal.'

'Anna says you fix everything.' She gazed into my face with a look of childlike trust that was quite at odds with the room we were standing in: the rumpled sheets, the silk underskirt, the atmosphere of illicit sex.

I smiled and promised to do my best.

When I left a few minutes later, having checked through the rest of the flat, she was kneeling beside M. Bertrand once more, crying. She didn't even glance at me. For a good-time girl she certainly seemed to be taking her loss to heart.

Blown helplessly this way and that back across the carpark, I began the return journey to our *gardien* flat through a blizzard that was worse than ever. The rough path I'd dug out before was all but covered. Our VW rustbox was a small mound of hardly visible whiteness. Daylight seemed to come from the deep snow rather than from above. Where had the sky gone? And the horizon? On all sides there was falling snow, and beyond that... nothing.

It was like crossing an ocean with no land in sight. At the halfway point, I felt like I was in the middle of nowhere. No sound but the rush and tearing roar of the wind, no landmarks: no up, down, left or right. Even the apartment blocks had disappeared. I had come from one and not yet reached the other – the past and the future, which was which?

A lifetime later, I came in sight of our block.

10

My *gardien* workshop was one of the best perks of the job. A vast improvement on the cardboard banana-box of tools I kept on top of the wardrobe in Edinburgh: here, at Les Montagnes Blanches, the saws sawed, the chisels chiselled and anything needing to be replaced was charged to the owners.

I laid out Thérèse's necklace on the workbench next to Anna's broken cassette player, then searched round for some emery paper, a soldering iron, a stick of fluxite. Repairing the necklace itself would take only a few minutes. I tried the drawers first, then rummaged through the cupboards. Anna's cassette player would have to be bumped down to second place in the queue, but only briefly. I'd been at the thing for over a month: fiddling about with it, laying it aside, then fiddling about with it again. I would mean to get back to it, then I'd forget. The last time we had climbed into the rustbox she'd said, 'Fancy some music?' – and then I'd *remembered*. Remembered that I'd forgotten yet again. Anna led the therapeutic Q & A session that followed, and helped pass the time all the way down to St-Ciers and back up again afterwards. The shortened version of the catechism went something like this: I forgot deliberately – because then there would always be something needing to be fixed, needing to be *healed*. Fixing things was a substitute for fixing (*healing*) myself. No one can heal until they start to feel the pain. I didn't want to feel the pain. And so on, and so on...

But on our next trip I planned to give her a real surprise. At first I'd pretend to be shocked, mortified even, to dicover her cassette player was still broken, that once again I'd *forgotten*. She'd get herself into analytical gear while I fiddled with the dial. Then – with a quick flick of the wrist – Michael Jackson would be with us, loud and clear as if he was moonwalking up and down the back seat. A triumph for Mr FixIt over Mr Freud.

Having found the soldering iron in an overhead cupboard, I was just lifting it down when the door opened. Quickly, I tossed an old rag on to the workbench, hoping to cover everything as best I could, including Thérèse's necklace. I grabbed a pair of pliers and waved them round busily.

'Some tea, Jack?'

Enter an outstretched mug of tea and a smile, followed by Anna herself. Very quietly, she closed the door behind her.

'Great, thanks. Just finishing off something. Nearly there.'

But she wasn't really listening. 'Poor Thérèse,' she began, 'so young, so alone, her mother and stepfather far away in Spain, she told me. Her father's dead, and there's no other family.' She shook her head. 'And now this.'

I put down the pliers, picked up the tea and drank.

'Almost an orphan,' she added.

'She's nearly seventeen.'

'Which makes her still only sixteen. Anyway, we had a good chat together, she and I...' Anna was beaming, truly beaming. 'She's a child really. A wee lass.'

What did that make me, then – the man with the bag of sticky sweets? At least Anna didn't seem to be jealous. Surprisingly.

I hadn't seen her so happy in ages. Excited, yes. Ecstatic even. In the relatively short time we'd been together, Anna had taken me to heights that were utterly mind-blowing – sexual highs I'd never known before, and emotional highs that made me feel more alive and passionately in love than I'd ever believed possible. But Anna happy – simply and straight-forwardly happy? Not like this. Not for months.

'As for that baby snatcher with his big red car and his penthouse, she's better off without him. I don't want to speak ill of the dead, Jack, especially when I never even met the man, but – a sixteen-year-old! Just a wee lassie!' She flicked her hair back and looked ten years younger, nearly. 'When I think of myself at that age! We worried about our homework, our boyfriends and our spots. It's a different world now – and she's all on her own.'

'She certainly seems pretty upset.'

'So you agree?'

'Agree to what?'

'That she's… that she's in danger. Aids for a start. And, anyway, her lifestyle.' She paused, then looked at me. 'And if *we* don't help her, chances are she won't be alone for long.'

'Well…' I began.

'Just for a few weeks, Jack.' That look on Anna's face, as if her whole happiness was awaiting only one word from me to be complete.

'Well…'

'She could stay here, with us. It would give her a chance to think things through, get herself a bit sorted.'

I reached forward to stroke Anna's hair and ease myself into diplomacy mode. 'A good idea, Anna. Let's talk about it tonight.'

She drew back. 'You don't want us to be happy together.'

'No, no. I didn't mean that.' I hesitated. 'It's a big step. We need to talk things through fully. We need to be quite sure we know precisely what would be involved and understand all the implications – for us and *between* us – before saying or doing anything.' A neatly worded bluster of a bodyswerve, in the circumstances.

Footsteps were coming along the hall. Perfect timing.

Thérèse walked in.

She greeted us and immediately asked after her necklace.

Anna turned to me. 'Fixing something for Thérèse now, are you?'

I knew that tone of voice only too well. Because, of course, I'd forgotten to mention to Anna the little favour I was doing for Thérèse – 'forgotten' in the analytical *deep-down* sense, no doubt.

'Just about to.' I slid the rag to one side, enough to uncover the necklace and repair tools. 'Only take a few minutes.' I turned and stared out of the window. Maybe I'd see a miracle out there. Maybe once I looked back again everything would be all right.

And when I turned round a few seconds later, the miracle had actually happened: in my absence it seemed that everyone had shifted into 'instant-family' mode. At least the two women had. Daughter Thérèse had picked up the silver chain from the workbench and was holding it towards me in her outstretched hand, the little-girl-hopefulness look on her face, while Mother Anna stood at her side, proud and indulgent. The pressure to be Fix-everything Father was being directed at me in stereo.

From Anna: our little girl's toy's broken – you can mend it and make her happy again.

From Thérèse: you're so strong and know how to do everything.

And me? The script must have been already written, so

effortlessly did I say my words: 'Give it here, then, and let's see what I can do.'

Thérèse and Anna stepped closer to see this mystery of reparation being performed for the benefit of everyone concerned. It was the Family Trinity I was soldering together.

All at once I became an onlooker. I watched the caring and capable father figure at work, leaning over his big workbench. I watched the mother and daughter standing one at each side of him. Seldom had my hands moved so surely and efficiently: get the soldering iron heated, lift the chain for a closer examination, place the broken ends together, a rub with the emery paper, a quick breath to blow away any dust, check the soldering iron's ready, a touch on the fluxite, a dab, joining together, a gentle breath to cool it down, a wipe, hold for a few seconds, place it down carefully.

At every perfectly executed stage I was so very aware of Thérèse on my right and couldn't but help remembering the sight of her loose night dress from the night before. To my left was Anna.

If there's love, there's jealousy; and when there's family, jealousy usually comes first.

'Well done, Jack. Real invisible mending!' said Anna.

'Thank you, thank you!' said Thérèse a split second later, and, for the very first time, she smiled at me.

Anna laid a proprietorial hand on my arm and gave me an affectionate, proprietorial squeeze. She was on a high – a mother superior with wings. She beamed. 'We should have a drink to celebrate!'

Without specifying exactly what we were celebrating, she left us and went to get the necessaries.

The moment we were alone, Thérèse pointed to where I'd

pulled aside the rag – a small corner of the cassette player was exposed.

'What's that, Jack?'

Was it my imagination or had she waited until Anna had gone before using my name?

Like a magician performing a conjuring trick, I whipped back the cover: 'Sshhh! Can you keep a secret? It's Anna's cassette player. It's broken, but I'm mending it. To surprise her.'

I put the rag back over it.

'Anna's a lucky woman,' Thérèse whispered, and the glance she gave me made the cheap trick seem worthwhile.

11

On that first evening in the bar of the Café Royal, when she had told me that she'd been an 'accident', I was sympathetic. Abandoned at birth, then getting passed from one set of foster parents to the next – it was a terribly sad story. I was *very* sympathetic. Afterwards, to lighten things up a little – it was our first date, after all – I commented, glibly: 'I suppose you could say that by getting born we're all "accidents" really. When you think about it.'

'And do you?'

'Do I what?'

'Think about it?'

Then she went on to ask me if I was pleased with the way things were working out for me. I grinned and replied that I'd had a happy childhood and had been drifting happily through life ever since. I was a happy person. There'd been school, then dropping out of college after a couple of terms, a few jaunts abroad between short-term money-raisers like being a security guard, storeman, courier, handyman. My light-hearted C.V. was then brought up to date with what I jokingly referred to as the high point of my existence: meeting her. I paused to allow her the chance to appreciate my graceful compliment. Instead, she leaned towards me.

'Did you really have a happy childhood?'

I nodded. 'Yeah, it was great. I loved my parents and they loved me.' I'd been just about to reveal the one major thing in my life that hadn't worked out when I felt the touch of her hand:

'Are you sure, Jack? Then how come you're just drifting?' She gave me a compassionate smile, and I melted.

'I'm happy – drifting.'

'Really?'

The more I insisted, the more she smiled her compassionate smile, and the more I melted.

From then on, and in the most loving way possible, Anna was always trying to sort me out, and I was always trying to stop her. By the time we first met Thérèse, we were well and truly jammed together in the doorway of self-development. Going nowhere – except for the incredible highs, and lows.

By the following morning the storm had finally blown itself out and I woke to complete silence and clear skies: a patch of blue showed through a gap in the curtains. In the half-light I could see the shadow of Anna's head on the pillow, a few blonde strands across her face. She looked at peace.

Completely snowed in, we were surrounded by utter silence: no wind, no birdsong, no movement of life whatever. It felt like the stillness of the enchanted palace in the fairy story where the sleeping princess would one day be awoken by her prince's kiss. Every few moments, Anna's eyelids flickered then settled again as she half-breathed, half-sighed to herself but remained asleep.

Without waking her, I eased myself out from under the downie, picked up my clothes from the chair and in a series of stealthy steps made for the bedroom door.

'Where are you going?' The princess had awoken.

I turned round. 'I'm off to see what I can do with the heating so that the place will be warm for you when you get up.' I smiled. 'All part of the service.'

She was sitting up in bed. She shook the hair from her face, then in a husky sex-goddess tone of voice called: 'Come back to bed, lover. You're all the heating I need.'

Her bed-warmth languor, her still-drowsy lasciviousness, her nakedness, her teasing lustfulness – those were the right buttons to press, and she was pressing them. I stood clutching my shirt and trousers and could already feel things stirring and stiffening down below. Standing there in our bedroom of Les Montagnes Blanches, trapped in an icebound wilderness, I played out the prince and princess fairy tale: I leaned near, kissed her and told her I loved her.

She laughed. 'Back into bed then – and show me!'

'The storm's stopped. I need to check on things. I'll be back as quick as anything. The generator— '

'You make it sound like an excuse.' She sighed and slumped back on to the pillow.

'Excuse for what?'

'For walking out.'

'Walking out? Christ, Anna, I'm only going to see to the generator so the heating won't— '

'Yes, yes. You've already told me that one. I'm talking about your walking out on me; this is a practice, even if you don't know it.'

Suddenly angry, I took a step towards the bed. 'You think you know fucking everything, don't you?'

'Knowing more than you do is hardly knowing everything, Jack, but I try my best.' She resettled her pillow to make herself more comfortable. 'You should try too – save me from always having to work things out for the both of us.'

'I'm going to turn up the heating, that's all. There's no hidden meaning.'

'No.' She nodded. 'The meaning's pretty clear.'

'There's no fucking meaning,' I shouted. My hands were trembling as I pulled on my trousers.

She hissed back at me: 'Keep your voice down, Jack. Thérèse is sleeping next door.'

'Never mind Thérèse,' I managed to say quietly before getting louder again. 'I'm going down to the basement to get the place heated up – right? Then I'll test the phone line – right? A walk round to check on any damage, clear a path, look at the car radiator.' I was so bloody furious I could hardly speak, never mind get my shirt buttoned.

She sat up. 'If you can get angry and let your anger out, it'll help both of us.'

I said nothing. I pulled on my jersey and turned to face her.

Then all at once, and to my complete surprise, I felt tears starting up behind my eyes. My voice began to choke. 'I love you, Anna, but how can we carry on living together when you never let up, not for a moment?' I was almost in tears. 'You just don't give an inch.'

'Jack, I don't have an inch to give.'

Next instant she was out of bed and had picked up a pair of scissors lying on the dressing table. Flourishing them as if they were a pointed knife, she turned them towards her. 'Why don't you just kill me and get it over with?'

'For fuck's sake, Anna! Don't be so— '

'Come on.' She took a step towards me. 'Come on. One good stab and all your problems will be over. You'll be a free man.'

'Anna! I love you, I'm not going to— '

'Will I make it easy for you?' She held the scissors to her stomach, pressing the sharp tip against her bare skin. 'Do I even have to do this for you?'

I made a grab for her hand. She fell backwards. Using all my strength, I tried to pull the scissors away. She wouldn't let them go. I dragged her across the top of the bed and on to the floor. For several seconds we lay quite still, getting our breath back.

This was the woman I loved, I told myself. I was trying to save her. Her face was hardly recognisable because of the scalding tears, the red-lined skin, the bared teeth, the spittle. The ugliness of her pain showed in every wrench and collapse of her mouth.

Then, like a storm passing as quickly as it had come, she became quite still and calm. I could feel her relax. I eased my grasp but didn't remove my hand, letting it remain there, covering hers but more gently.

'Jack, Jack.' She sighed. All the rage had gone from her.

'I'm sorry. I didn't mean to...' She leaned towards me, whispering tenderly, almost caressingly. She let go the scissors and they slipped on to the carpet beside us.

She clung to me and began weeping deep, racking sobs. She put her lips to the back of my hand. Drawing her mouth tenderly and lovingly over my skin, she began kissing me, licking me...

We were back to the familiar craziness/forgiveness/megafuck cycle. An ecstatic high – solid ground once more.

After we made love we remained on the floor. Through the gap in the curtains the chill light from outside became gradually brighter.

As I lay there I could feel everything around us freezing into position – in the room and in the landscape outside. And at the centre of it all were the two of us locked in each other's arms.

12

I remember reading somewhere that the centre of hell is supposed to be a frozen lake where the damned are held fast for ever – unable to feel anything, unable to move. That was us, all right. But in time, around Les Montagnes Blanches at least, the weather changed. With the end of the storm, the sun began to shine, the snow to melt.

The phone worked again. I contacted head office and told them about M. Bertrand. The following morning a local *département* snowplough cleared its way from the village up to the car park, and immediately behind it came an ambulance and the police. Anna and I were questioned. M. Bertrand's body was removed for further examination. Just routine, they said. It was clear that he'd died by slipping on the snow and ice, falling and striking his head on the balcony tiles. 'Real bad luck,' they said. Bad luck, all right. M. Bertrand would be buried in Paris. His Ferrari was removed to a local garage, to remain there until all the formalities had been completed.

Thérèse wanted to leave, so we drove her down to the station and said goodbye.

So much for the short-term happy family. Anna was genuinely sorry to see her go. When we returned, we found the police waiting for us in M. Bertrand's apartment. More formalities, they explained: the penthouse now had to be sealed and, as I was the only company representative at the scene, I had to sign as the official witness.

Everything completed, Anna went back to our flat while I accompanied the two *gendarmes* to their car. They were about to drive off when one of them rolled down his window and beckoned me over.

'Was maybe even her own father, can you beat that? Still a bit unclear, but looks like it.'

'What?'

'Bloody Parisians, eh! *Ciao.*'

I was too surprised even to reply.

Once they'd driven off, I stood for several minutes trying to take in what I'd just been told. Her *father*, for Christ's sake. Her own father. It couldn't have been. The *gendarme* was joking, wasn't he? Young girl and older man – that was all.

Or was it? For a good-time girl she'd seemed pretty

devastated. But... Thérèse and her own father? M. Bertrand and his own daughter? Neither made sense.

I stared at the car park and beyond. Sunlight was lying in streaks across the melting snow and puddles; stripped of their white covering, the trees looked like meaningless scribbles on the white of the mountainsides.

13

Hearing that Thérèse, the 'wee lassie', might have been shacked up with her own father seemed to finish everything for Anna. That, or the sudden thaw. Around us, the world dripped, splashed and gurgled. Colours began to show through the thinning crust of ice and snow: patches of green, grey asphalt, brown branches. Overnight, winter was over.

The following evening Anna announced she'd pretty much had it with the majestic scenery, the Jacuzzi picnics, the multi-channel TV, the limitless hot water. She wanted a home, she said, a real home. With me, or without.

We'd just sat down to dinner together – roast venison, three veg, two bots and one carving knife – when the romantic candlelit interrogation began:

Didn't I want to get married one day? Have children?

'Well...' I stalled.

She grabbed my hand and held it a bit too near the candle flame.

Had we a real future together?

'Of course we have.' I shook myself free and blew on my

palm to cool it down.

And marriage? Children?

As a joke I made a show of pulling both my hands safely out of her reach.

She smiled and said she'd only been pretending. 'How's the poor little boy's hand?'

I held it out to get it kissed better. She took it. She kissed it. Did I accept her apology? she asked. She'd just been pretending, that was all. She leaned across and smiled.

Just pretending, because what she'd really meant to do was...

This time I wasn't quick enough.

A flash of sharpened silver by candlelight and she'd picked up the carving knife and was turning the blade against herself. Next moment she'd fallen forward, her head crashed down on to the table. Her glass was knocked over; her hair and her face lay in a pool of '85 Margaux. She didn't move.

'Anna! Anna!' I grabbed her shoulder to pull her up. 'Anna! For Christ's sake!'

There was no response. The knife was somewhere underneath her.

Very, very carefully I lifted her: the blondeness of her hair was soaked blood-red, her eyes were closed.

'Anna!'

Not a sound, not a flicker of life.

I was kneeling at her side, psyching myself up to raise her head a little more. She might be dying. She might even be dead.

'Gave you a fright, did I?' She grabbed hold of my arm.

Gripping me tighter, she hauled herself up straight. The carving knife clattered back on to the table as bright, unmarked and shiny as before. She'd been pretending. Or rather, as she explained it, she'd been showing me how devastated I would feel to lose her. That was all.

I went back to my seat.

She'd just been making a point, she said. She reached over and touched me lightly on the wrist and added that it was time we both had a change of scene. We were ready to move on, weren't we? Then she smiled, righted her glass and poured refills.

Moments later she was detailing our shared future. She pointed out that just because the world was slipping into terrorist hands, thanks to Bush and Blair, there was no reason we shouldn't make a home for ourselves – a safe place where we could be together, whatever happened. She offered me a compromise: she agreed to stay for a few months longer on the understanding that we'd start to save like crazy, get ourselves enough money to make a mortgage downpayment towards a a place of our own. No more renting, no more living in other people's houses. The first rung on the property ladder, she said. It'd take a few thousand, as Edinburgh was getting very expensive. She set a deadline. Back there for the beginning of August – holiday time would be best, she explained, before prices went up again in the autumn. We'd get a flat of our own and a real job; we'd get married and start a family. We would begin to live in the real world.

14

We gave in our notice on 30 June. Our final cheques were paid into the bank on 31 July, and we celebrated our last day with a farewell liberation from the cellars, then loaded up the rustbox. We were ready to leave.

The VW shuddered, stalled and panted all the way to Paris, where we sold it to a hard-nosed auto-pirate for scrap. Too late to get an EasyJet seat. A few days in Gay Paree first? Not Anna. Douce Edinburgh – she couldn't wait. First stop: an Internet café to download a few dozen pages from the Edinburgh Solicitors' Property Centre website – reading material for the journey home.

Next stop, the Gare du Nord.

Noise, dirt, the din of loudspeakers, the crowds – and the two of us like a couple of marmots down from the mountains with our suitcases, rucksacks and overnight bags.

We buy our tickets, find the Eurostar train. We get on.

While she's settling herself in her seat – with the ESPC printouts already to hand – Anna's chattering and laughing, as high as a kite. Not that she lets past my casual jest about travelling through the tunnel being a bit Freudian. At once, the Big A crops up. Once we're back, she suggests, why don't I sign up for my very own three analytical evenings per week? We could go out together afterwards and talk through our respective sessions over a drink.

Despite my being to all appearances a fully paid-up passenger in a high-speed train, I recognise that I am at a crossroads in my life – and the traffic lights are about to turn red. Only a few seconds on amber remain.

I'm reaching for one of the bottles of Lafite, a parting gift from the *cave* of M. Dubois, that innocent philanthropist. The train's about to go.

The amber is flickering.

The departure warning sounds – and I'm still holding my overnight bag.

'Look who's come to see us off!' I point towards the platform.

She turns round to peer out of the window. 'Who? Who? Where?' She's straining to see.

'I'll get them at the door,' I call out, rushing off down the carriage.

I got out just in time. Behind me, the train was beginning to pick up speed. Orpheus may have made a hash of things when he left the underworld, but I was damned sure I wasn't going to: even if Anna banged on the window or started shouting, there was going to be no backward glance from me. Not that I intended hanging around to give her the chance. Overnight bag in one hand, Lafite in the other, I went hoppity-skippity-jump up the platform towards the station concourse. Behind me, Anna and all her problems were Eurostarring out of my life at 150mph with no stop this side of the Channel.

Straight to the Café du Nord for a celebratory *demi*.

Poor Anna.

A few sips later I was reassuring myself that she was better off without me. I tried not to picture her waiting for me to come back into the carriage. I tried not to imagine her growing doubts, then her tears, her fury. It would be getting on for the rush hour as she struggled up and down the endless corridors and stairs of the London Underground. It would be dark by the time she arrived in Edinburgh. She'd have to get out of the train alone; she'd have to deal with her suitcase and rucksack – assuming she'd abandoned mine en route. Where would she stay? With foster parents number three?

Poor Anna.

I emptied my glass.

One thing was sure: there'd be no more talking things through all night, no more screaming and raging, no more biting, scratching and stabbing. I had survived. Life's traffic lights were glimmering green again.

Two *demis* later I headed off to explore Paris.

August 2003

1

The Louvre, the Seine, Notre-Dame. The boulevards, the cafés, the parks. Hot sun and warm shade. Short skirts, summer dresses, high heels. Long hair, bare shoulders, breasts, midriffs, thighs, eye contact and smiles. Enough money to last three months and more, enough French to follow up the eye contacts, to chat up the smiles...

I lasted three days.

Three very lonely days. The Louvre, the Seine, Notre-Dame. Sitting alone at café tables, sitting alone on park benches. The wrong city? The wrong girls? The wrong me?

The Iraq War might be officially over, but the rest of the world was hardly feeling a safer place. Paris in particular. The city seemed to be overrun by armed police on the lookout for terrorists. Security teams, usually in bulletproof jackets and carrying sub-machine guns, patrolled the railway stations, the corridors of the Métro and even the carriages themselves, accompanied by savage-looking Alsatians straining at the leash. Police and their vans were everywhere. Most of all, they targeted the streets and small squares of the immigrant quarter lying just beyond the overhead Métro at Barbès-Rochechouart and known as la Goutte d'Or.

Darkness was falling one evening when, after walking for what seemed like kilometres, I ended up there. Thanks to a dutiful thank-you letter she'd written after leaving us, I knew Thérèse's address. Maybe I should look her up? Make sure she was recovering after her tragic loss. No need to mention that I was aware M. Bertrand might possibly have been her father. No need to say anything except hello and take it from there.

Her address was a cul-de-sac of parked cars and lack of sunlight. It would have been really dismal but for the lively clutter of shops with rolls of brightly coloured fabrics out on the pavement, food stalls selling falafel and hot chickens turning on spits, café windows stacked high with bright red, green and yellow sweets. Every few metres I had to step on to the road to avoid bumping into groups of North African-looking men standing around and talking in what was probably Arabic. I couldn't help noticing that quite a few of them were Bin Laden lookalikes, near enough. Dangerous? Exotic? Definitely not touristland. I was obviously a stranger, but no one seemed to mind.

The street door was open. I walked up to the fourth floor and rang. There was no reply. I rang again, and was about to leave when the door finally opened.

Dressed in jeans, an off-white T-shirt logoed UNIVERSITÉ DE NANTERRE and in bare feet, Thérèse looked as if she'd just got out of bed. Her rainbow-coloured hair was drab and straggly. The girl I'd met in the mountains had been chic, a

Ferrari-driven penthouse playgirl. No Ferrari and no penthouse was the least of it.

The apartment was mostly windowless corridor. We went into the main room. Though not large, at one time it would have been a modest family salon with its elegant mirror, gilt-framed, set above the fireplace and French windows leading onto the small balcony above the street. Nowadays it was a no man's land of weary-looking furniture, clothes scattered everywhere, drawers hanging half-open; a pair of audio speakers sat on a sideboard, unconnected wires dangling like multi-coloured creeper-weed; the carpet crunched underfoot. A bit of work and the place could have been really quite smart, but Thérèse had clearly given up on it. The mirror's curved gilt beading was chipped and flaking off; clouded with grease, spotted with dirt and cracked in one corner, the glass had clearly lost heart reflecting the dismal scene it was faced with.

'Some wine?' I flourished the bottle of red I'd brought.

A couple of clean-looking glasses were found.

'*Santé!*' I toasted, and we drank.

I moved a pile of unwashed clothes and sat down on the couch. She slouched in the armchair opposite. Between us was a very smeary coffee table littered with dirty dishes, plastic throwaway cutlery, mugs of unfinished coffee, empty pizza cartons. I cleared a space for my glass.

She asked after Anna, and I said that we had separated.

After nearly half a minute's silence she replied: 'Anna is a good woman. I like her.'

'She has gone back to Scotland.'

'You are missing her?'

'Hmmm...' I gave a half-nod, half-shake of my head to

suggest agreement and regret. Then I quickly moved on. 'So, Thérèse, how are you?'

She shrugged. She managed a smile. 'OK. I live.'

It was going to be hard work. After another sip I topped up our glasses.

'I wanted to come to see you.'

She fingered the chain round her neck, from time to time touching the silver crescent-moon pendant. She stroked it absently. Another half-smile. 'You see me.'

'Yes, so I do. And I'm very pleased to be here.'

After a half-hour's chat, with me doing most of the chatting, about Paris, about the Louvre, the Seine and Notre-Dame; about the boulevards, the cafés, the parks; about the armed police; about wanting to come to see her but being uncertain if I should – we had finished the bottle.

There was another pause between us.

From out in the street I heard a lorry reversing the length of the cul-de-sac. When the engine whine died away, I leaned forward: 'That necklace you're wearing – it's the one I mended for you, isn't it?'

'My father gave it to me.'

For a brief moment I was back in that bedroom in the Alpine penthouse. The rumpled bed, the discarded nightdress...

2

I hadn't planned on staying with Thérèse; I just didn't leave. After several nights on the couch of her dishevelled living room, I moved into her dishevelled bedroom. She seemed pleased enough to have me in her bed and in her life. Glad of the company, perhaps. I know I was. We got on well enough together, in a non-demanding sort of way. No great highs, but no great lows either. From the start it was a low-maintenance relationship.

Living with Thérèse was like heaven after hell: she didn't want to make me a better person; she didn't want me to get in touch with my inner feelings/my childhood/my masculinity/ my femininity/my real self. She didn't finish my sentences, explain my jokes or interpret my dreams. We'd make love and then, without a post-coital debriefing to analyse what had been learned from the experience, we'd fall asleep. She looked her real age – eighteen. She'd lied to Anna or, as she put it, not corrected Anna's mistaken assumption: 'She wanted a little girl. I made her happy.'

Her bedroom was tiny and mostly bed – a double mattress on the floor. It was a nest where we spent most of our time. The morning after we first slept together, we lay side by side on top of the duvet. While I read more than fifty pages of sci-fi she stared up at the ceiling, half-dozing, as I thought.

All at once, and without turning round to face me, she spoke. 'When you come here you say you remember my necklace, then we kiss for the first time. Yes?'

'Ah, yes, I remember it well,' I half-sang in a mock-Maurice Chevalier voice.

She waited until I had finished my impersonation, then added: 'It was a present from my *real* father, not my step-father. I have told you?'

I nodded, encouraging her to go on.

She didn't.

*

We had enough money. No rent. She had inherited the flat from her father – all that was left of an expensive lifestyle, it seemed. As the place was too dingy to be tidied up in one go, we didn't even try. Most mornings we stayed in the nest, afternoons we wandered the streets. Sometimes the weather belonged more to a Scottish summer than a French one: dry, warm days that would be suddenly set shivering by a cold wind that sent us into the nearest café. We must have walked the whole of central Paris: the Left Bank, the Tuileries, the old town of the Marais, up and down the steep cobbled slopes of Montmartre. Evenings, we ate locally in cheap restaurants – North African cafés with single men eating off trays: chicken and rice, merguez and rice, lamb curry and rice. If we wanted some brightness and bustle we went to a McDonald's. Another day, another dinner. Then back home, up the stairs, close the front door, and into the nest.

The phone never rang. It was several days before I realised the connection had been pulled out. I never asked and she never explained. Why go looking for problems? I'd had more than enough question-and-answer sessions with Anna. Thérèse was just a quiet girl. Fine. Suited me. Quietness, it seemed, was what we both needed for the time being. This pause in our lives, this convalescence almost, was where we belonged. After Anna, I was very grateful for the change.

One evening, a month to the day after I had turned up on her doorstep, Thérèse suggested we should have a big night out together to celebrate: we would get dressed up and dine in a real restaurant. Somewhere very French, with good food, lots of people and noise, not expensive either – not 'snob-chic, snob-*cher'*, as she put it. And she knew just the place.

Before we left we gave our big-night-out look a last-minute check. For me, clean shirt and clean jeans; for Thérèse, a lowish-cut, silvery-blue summer dress with spaghetti straps and a tasselled silk shawl for when the evening turned cool. We stood side by side in front of the defeated-looking mirror as Thérèse applied a final hint of eye-shadow and a last touch of lipstick. She leaned close to the glass. She drew the light pink carefully over her lips, then inspected the result. Hers was a most serious inspection that was rounded off, eventually, with a very pleased and sponta-neous grin.

I made her laugh out loud by reaching my hand towards the mirror, as if wanting a kiss from her freshly painted lips' reflection. Instead, she turned and kissed me lightly on the cheek. When she moved, I was left with my hand still pressed on the glass. Briefly, I felt as if I was steadying my own image. So I stood back and pretended to straighten an invisible tie. Thérèse picked up her handbag, and off we went.

A twenty-minute stroll through the early-evening sunlight, easy and downhill for the length of Rue de Rochechouart, past cafés with pavement tables, all seats taken for pre-dinner apéritifs, then on to Rue Cadet, where the last of the market stalls were being cleared. Once in the Rue du Faubourg-Montmartre the restaurant smells – Lebanese, Moroccan, Italian, French – hurried us forward. There was a spring in our step. Thérèse took my arm. We chattered about menus, about the shops and people we passed, about the fish market, the falafel stalls, what we'd eat, the wine we'd drink. Like the first date we'd never had.

Chartier's restaurant turned out to be full; every table was taken. We joined a queue that snaked out through the revolving doors into the courtyard. Somewhere else? I suggested.

'Many people here because it is a good place. We do not wait long. You will see. No one has reservation here. No worries.'

Less than ten minutes later a man in a dark suit and black bow tie showed us into a booming barn of a place that was a cross between a Toulouse-Lautrec poster of waistcoated waiters with turn-of-the-century moustaches, white aprons, armfuls of plates, Art Deco wood and stained glass – and a Victorian railway station, minus the trains. Diners were accommodated often at least six to a table. Our seats faced each other, the middle two in a table with seating for ten. Our immediate neighbours were already well into their respective meals. We greeted them with a *bonsoir*, and sat down. Within seconds the waiter appeared.

For me, garlic snails and *oeuf au cheval* with chips. For Thérèse, a plate of *langoustines* and *salade niçoise*. The waiter scribbled our order down on the paper tablecloth and rushed off. Moments later he was back with cutlery, a basket of cut-up *baguette*, two wine glasses and a bottle of the house red. To our immediate left, our elbows almost touching, was a couple who were clearly on their first date. She was French and he was Spanish, their common language was English. They spoke shyly, almost in whispers. To our right, a French couple: he talked and didn't eat, she ate and didn't talk. I poured out our wine. We toasted a happy evening together, and drank.

Our food arrived. '*Bon appétit!*'

I picked up my knife and fork. For Thérèse, however, *langoustines* were a hands-on event. Rip off the head, rip off the tail, and a fingernail up the belly to push back the legs.

Then strip off the shell.

She bit into the white flesh. 'Mmm. *Très délicieux!* Very, very good taste. You like? You not like?' She ripped off another tail. 'You like better the head? Yeuch!' Little-girl disgust, then a little-girl smile as she picked up the next one and pretended she was going to toss it into the air. 'Heads or tails?'

But instead of eating it she laid down her *langoustine* and took a sip of wine. When she replaced her glass on the table there was a lipstick smudge on the rim. I found myself staring at it, fascinated. For several seconds I was aware of that trace of pale pink, so intense, as if it was the only thing still remaining in the world.

For no reason at all I felt quite certain that when I raised my eyes to where she was sitting, there would be no Thérèse opposite me, and never had been. That trace of lipstick was my only proof. I wanted to reach forward to touch it, to prove... what? That there was an actual world around me, that I was *somewhere*? That I was not utterly alone?

A moment later I glanced back at Thérèse. I smiled at her. She smiled back, clearly a little puzzled at my silence – she was waiting for me, it seemed, to respond to some remark she'd just made.

To my surprise I heard myself say: 'I think I've fallen in love with you.'

Next thing, she had taken my hand and lifted it to her mouth. She kissed it.

'Love?' she asked.

3

One morning a few days later I was woken by Thérèse telling me she had to go out but would be back soon. I was to wait. Sure thing. But where was she going?

She laid a finger on my lips to silence me.

Shortly afterwards I heard the front door slam. She had gone.

Fresh *croissants* for breakfast, perhaps? Very welcome they'd be too. I dozed off to the sound of an Arabic pop song coming up from the street, to frequent shouts, car horns, traffic.

At 10.25 a.m. by the bedside clock I heard her return.

The bedroom door was thrown open, and the curtains pulled back to let in the mid-morning.

'For you and for me.' Thérèse was waving two white envelopes in the air. 'Catch!'

Mine landed on the pillow. Before I could pick it up, she'd jumped on to the bed and was kneeling in front of me, her hand covering the packet. Like taking my turn in the kids' game, I immediately put my left hand on hers, then she placed hers on mine, and lastly I pressed my right one down to hold the pillar steady.

'A present?'

'Ssh!' She leaned forward, her hair falling like a rainbow-coloured screen behind which she kissed my hand. When she sat up again, she looked very serious. Not little-girl serious either. 'You don't want, you say and you can cash in.' She paused, bit her lip. 'And... and... and all is finished.'

We lifted back our hands one at a time. Without saying anything more, she gave me the envelope and watched me open it.

*

An hour later we were walking up the steep climb of Rue des Martyrs to Place des Abbesses and then on to Montmartre. Artistland for tourists. The weather had suddenly changed: a chill wind, a grey sky patched with watery-looking clouds and a wintry-looking sun spattering weak colours on the grey pavements and cobbles of the Place du Tertre. The cafés surrounding the square were packed and their windows steamed up with condensation. The pavement artists were well wrapped up, some of them busy giving instant portraits in charcoal, while others sat on camp stools and had their various *scènes de Paris* set out for sale on small tables, on easels or tied to railings. For authenticity, some dabbed an occasional spot of colour here and there on to an oil-smeared canvas. The outdoor café tables and chairs were puddled from the most recent downpour.

We walked a little further, eventually sitting down at the very top of the steps that lead up to the church of Sacré-Coeur. From there, my coat under us to keep us dry, our arms round each other to keep us warm, we gazed out across the city spread below in all directions. The low cloud made the stone buildings and hints of blue sky far in the distance look like another *scène* that hadn't yet been sold. Despite the weather, there were tourists all round us – mostly British and German, not many Americans these days. A murmur of Japanese was posing and clicking its way down to a waiting bus. The steps were cold, and so were we. Thérèse shivered.

Then she explained about the rail ticket she'd given me. She told me about the wilderness in the mountains above Barcelona and about her friends Toni and Charlie – short for Charlotte – who had moved there after meeting in India.

'Hippies?'

'Kind of. But this is real. They build their houses, grow their food and live. Now I am ready, I want to go and visit them.'

It was a loose community, Thérèse said, a handful of houses built half a kilometre or so apart, the land itself being held in common. Charlie came originally from Australia and Toni from Spain. She'd met them when, after being in India, the two of them had come to find work in the Spanish resort on the Costa Dorada where she herself used to live. They were really good friends. 'Very kind,' she added, 'and I am ready for kindness now. With thanks to you, Jack.'

According to Thérèse, the couple now lived much the same easy-going existence in the wilderness as they had enjoyed when they first got together in Pondicherry – like a long holiday from some non-existent job elsewhere.

'You will come too, Jack? Yes?'

That was a moment of true togetherness on the steps of Sacré-Coeur, with Thérèse's voice just inches away, snuggled into the warmth of my coat, telling me about this laid-back paradise in Spain. About the wild horses, the heat, the clear water, the freedom. The kindness.

The following morning, while Thérèse met an agent to arrange getting the flat serviced and rented out, I went for a walk along the Boulevard de Rochechouart towards Pigalle. I walked up the wide tree-lined central section that had occasional stalls selling everything from T-shirts and fluffy toys to cheap batteries while the traffic roared up and down on either side. Ten minutes later I crossed Place Blanche and realised I'd wandered into the red-light district. Neon lights flashed off and on: *Hard Sex, Porno, Girls, Naked, Strip, Peepshow private – two euros*. Most of the signs were in English. International appeal. Just then I noticed, only a few metres to my right up a side-street, a line of women standing a couple of metres apart, several of them looking in my direction. The nearest, a blonde with letter-box lipstick, an overhanging cleavage, shiny yellow skirt and high heels, caught my eye and began making kissing noises. She leaned back against the wall and flicked her tongue at me. I looked away. She spat on the ground.

Moments later I was returning along the boulevard towards Barbès, thinking *city life* – but how very different a city from Edinburgh.

Edinburgh. A sudden stab of guilt. My mother.

It would be a long overdue phone call, as always.

Standing in the glass-walled *cabine* – the door closed to shut out the noise of cars and buses only a few metres away – I pictured her in her Edinburgh flat. When she hears the phone ringing she'll be at her worktable in the front room, up to her elbows in a midden of silks, scraps of lace and frayed thread, all the table leaves pulled out as she works away on the sewing machine that takes up the only clear space. Ever since my father died, the walls had been hung with half-finished garments; two dressmaker's dummies stood on either side of the blocked-up fireplace, a full-length mirror between them; my piano was heaped with lengths of coloured cloth and material waiting to be cut, spilling from the top on to the closed keyboard. The air was almost chewable with dust.

Now she's come into the hall, picked up the receiver.

'Hello. McCall's Alterations.' Her voice sounds tired.

After asking how she was and apologising for not phoning sooner, I told her where I was going. There was a long pause. 'Spain? Just for the weekend, then?'

'Well, I'm— '

'Anna comes to see me, at least. Nice lass. Been round a few times, she has.'

'Well— '

'Broke her heart you have, son.'

After five euros' worth we said goodbye and I hung up. I stared at the receiver. I imagined her shaking her head, then slipper-shuffling back to the front room to carry on with her work at the precise point where she'd been interrupted. The machine whirrs into action, the needle comes down like a cat's claw ripping into silk, just as it's done five times per second, ten hours a day, six days a week, ever since my father was buried.

I stepped out of the *cabine* into the noise of the boulevard once again. Never mind the endless traffic from Barbès, the stopping and starting, the horns and the metal screech of brakes – all I could hear was that relentless *prrrr* machine-stabbing at me like an accusatory finger.

For a few metres or so anyway.

Next day, Thérèse and I took our seats on the TGV to Barcelona.

4

It had happened on my thirteenth birthday.

For most of the winter our front room was never much above freezing, so I'd brought through a mug of tea that January morning and switched on the electric fire; the bars glowed, hissed and spat back at me before giving out a little heat. Darkness outside and with an east wind gusting rain against the window, rattling the glass panes for accompaniment, I sat down at the piano to start on some Czerny exercises. They'd get my chilled fingers moving: a burst of arpeggios blurring up and down the keyboard, then scales, major, minor, four-octave runs a third apart, contrary motion. No soul-searching interpretation, no subtle phrasing, just the same patterns repeated until the notes seemed to play themselves while I looked on.

That was me, the child prodigy: at five I'd played like a very gifted nine-year-old, at nine like a gifted twelve-year-old. In the evening I'd be giving a sort of short 'show-off' concert recital for my family and, most important of all, for Mr McAllister, the music adviser to Lothian region. Now I'd turned thirteen, my teacher, Mr Quin, was planning to enter me for the Leeds Piano Competition the following year. I'd be one of the youngest ever.

I lifted down the score of Bach's Italian Concerto and turned to the *Andante*. I played it through once, then played it through again. The singing melody, the measured bass line, the shifting harmonies. After weeks of practice I now had the entire piece note-perfect...

The whole family was there that evening, even deaf Uncle

Todd. They all believed in me.

I sat down and played. I gave it my best ever.

Afterwards I sat back, the applause breaking out before I'd even turned round to face everyone. Mr McAllister was clapping too.

He had to rush off – to catch the Glasgow train, he said. Before he left, he spoke to my parents.

'A fine pianist you've got there, Mr McCall – you must be very proud of him.'

My father shook the adviser's hand enthusiastically and nodded like his head would fall off. All the while he kept repeating, 'Yes! Yes, Mr McAllister! Thank you. He's a great lad. He'll go places.' He was blushing with pleasure and pride.

Three days later Mr Quin gave me the bad news.

We were in his bow-windowed Marchmont flat where I usually had my lessons. After he had spoken I just sat there at the piano looking across to him in his armchair, with the Bach score still spread open on his knees.

Like someone struggling to take their next breath, I strained for the sounds of something solid to hold on to – from outside there was the rumble of car tyres on the Spottiswoode Street cobbles, but it seemed to come from far, far away. I wanted to hear the faintly ticking clock on the mantelpiece, the slight hiss from the central heating radiator, the bustle of Mrs Quin unpacking her shopping through in the kitchen. But now there was only silence – as if I'd been struck deaf.

I remembered that birthday evening so clearly. I remembered Mr McAllister giving me a warm smile as he turned to my father. 'A fine pianist you've got there,' he'd said. Meaning it kindly, no doubt.

Speaking to Mr Quin in private, however, as I now learned, the music adviser had then added: 'The boy's a fine pianist, but not a *very* fine one.' Good, but not good enough.

I didn't understand. I knew I'd played well. I'd felt absolutely at one with Bach's music. Mr McAllister had praised me. He'd shaken my father's hand and had praised me.

Mr Quin said not to worry. Whatever happened, he reassured me, I would always be a musician, but maybe Leeds could wait a year; no sense in rushing things.

My parents, of course, noticed nothing. To them I was still the prodigy, the pride of the family. Studies and scales, studies and scales until, as my dad joked, they could have set the metronome by me rather than the other way round. Back from work, he'd stick his head round the side of the door. 'Keep going, son, we're loving it. We know you'll get there. We're proud of you.'

Until then we'd been the original Happy Family: Mr McCall the roofer, Mrs McCall his wife and Jack their child prodigy. Overnight I was no longer a child, no longer a prodigy. And going out of my fucking mind.

What was wrong? I was doing exactly as I'd always done. The correct notes, sensitive phrasing and intonation, expressive legato and so on, and so on... *A fine pianist, but not a very fine one*.

I began to panic.

At first, every morning's playing had me in tears. Then I got determined. Fuck them. I'd show them. That fucking adviser. Fucking Leeds Competition. Mr Quin.

I got up earlier, practised even harder. I played faster and faster as if trying to catch up with something far ahead of me. I played and played and played. Louder and louder. Before school, after school. Willpower kept me going, willpower and desperation. My hammering on the keys was like battering on a door that had been locked against me. Sometimes I hammered at it so hard the blood came seeping out from under my fingernails.

If you can imagine hell as a place where you played Mozart...

'That's the style, son. Keep at it. We're proud of you.'

Had I been given a gift only to have it taken away? Had there been no real gift in the first place?

Then something seemed to break inside me.

When my father died three years later, I wept – from sheer relief. I loved him, but his death removed the unbearable weight of his hopes, his expectations and his unshakeable belief. I felt happier than I'd felt in a long time.

With my father's death, I could stop playing. I slammed down the lid of the piano. And that was that.

If only Anna hadn't interrupted me that first evening in the bar of the Café Royal to put me right about happiness and Scottish childhoods...

She and her therapy-speak would have had a field day as she explained to me how my 'inner harmony', as she would probably have termed it, had been brought to an abrupt end coincident with the onset of my adolescence. The entire process – an expression of inner distress, of displaced sublimation let's call it – was triggered, with all the inevitability of Jungian synchronicity, by the particular manner and trauma of my father's death (i.e. his 'fall'), which (deep down) I had actually rejoiced over. But even though she would have gone on and on about it, I wish I had managed to tell her what had happened. Tell her everything.

Instead, it was Thérèse who heard the whole sad story. It helped pass some of the time on our high-speed train journey from Paris to Barcelona. I had hoped a similar confidence would have come from her – about her father.

It didn't.

5

It was late afternoon when we arrived at Barcelona's Sants station. As we walked along the platform and into the main hall, Thérèse mumbled something to me. But around us the noise was almost deafening: loudspeakers boomed announcements of trains, platform numbers, times of arrivals and departures to places all over Spain and abroad, fast-food stalls had their radios gabbling, thudding and jingling, TV screens were restless swirls of pop videos and adverts. I couldn't make out a word she'd said.

Then I thought I'd misheard.

She repeated it again.

'Your parents? We're going to be visiting your parents?'

'They will come to meet us.'

'We'll be staying with them, you mean?'

No response.

'Thérèse, why didn't you tell me?'

She turned to avoid my glance. 'Maybe you not want to visit them?'

'Maybe I'd liked to have been asked.'

'Yes. Maybe…'

Thérèse's parents were supposed to pick us up, and they

were late. We waited and waited. We nearly had our first row.

Thérèse's reasonable complaint: '*Maman* said she will come. She promised. It is two years since last time I was here. Two years since she saw me.' She was angry, she was almost in tears.

My reasonable response: 'Maybe we should just take the local train, then a taxi to their house?'

'And if she comes and we are not here? This will be a very bad start, I think.'

'What about phoning them? Find out if they're on their way?'

No response.

'I said, what about phoning...?'

No response.

Her parents arrived forty minutes late, her mother bristling with apologies about city traffic and tourists. At first glance Claudine was a nice-looking woman, unnaturally blonde, with her sunglasses worn on the hair like a pushed-up visor and, as I noticed when she embraced Thérèse, each hand fitted with a full set of blood-tipped nails. The straight man of the couple remained standing at a few metres' distance: a small, roundish forty-year-old in jeans, denim jacket, ironed white shirt and sensible shoes. He took a step forward and shook my hand.

'Pablo. Hello to you, Jack.'

Next, he greeted Thérèse in Spanish, shook her hand, then lifted up the bigger suitcase and went bumping off out to the car. His 'Welcome to Spain, Jack' as he switched on the ignition were to be his last words until we reached their home.

Mother and daughter sat in the back. Claudine called forward to me: 'We will try to speak English sometimes, Jack. Pablo has learned to speak many visitor languages.' She tapped my shoulder, 'Please correct every error. It is help for us to speak better.'

I said I would.

Within less than a minute she'd begun speaking French again. I switched off.

The Barcelona streets were a mayhem of taxi horns, shouts, screeching brakes and near collisions – Pablo drove through them with an alarming calmness. His hands set in a steady ten-to-two grip on the steering wheel and his eyes fixed on the road ahead, he ignored everything around him; when hooted or snarled at, he neither hooted nor snarled back. As we became part of the surge round the statue of Christopher Columbus, then cut across two lanes and peeled off to go roaring up the Ramblas, the only red car in a shoal of black and yellow taxis, I gripped the dashboard with one hand and the door handle with the other. A flick of his eye told me he had noticed my unease. He said nothing, which said it all.

We passed from two-lane streets crammed with traffic to a four-lane highway crammed with traffic. Forty minutes of high-speed, bumper-to-tail terror later, the four lanes were squeezed back to two. We were coming round the edge of the coast with a narrow strip of beach and the sea to our left. To our right was a never-ending strip of shops, bars and hotels with signs for *Restaurante*, *Apartamente*, *Club*, *Disco*. Every hundred metres or so we'd see a *Brown Cow Pub*, or *The Shamrock*, or *Jimmy and Jenny's*. The pavements seethed with shorts, sandals and sunburn. Early evening, but still warm. Very, very warm. My eyes were closing...

I was jerked awake, my seat belt clutching me tightly. The car had just braked to a sudden halt. Having presumably turned off the main road we were now in an area of hardly any through-traffic, white-walled blocks of flats and hotels lined both sides of the street, massive tourist coaches from Germany, Belgium and France, plus a couple from Britain, were parked nose-to-tail. Many of the balconies were draped with swimming costumes and brightly coloured beach towels. The pavements were shaded by palm trees. Pablo was waiting for a well-dressed Spanish woman to coax her small dog out of his road. The *señora*, red-faced, irritated and embarrassed, tugged at the lead; the dog ignored her and continued grooming itself. Pablo said nothing, did nothing. The passing seconds were marked by a tic-tic that had started up in the corner of his right eye. The woman looked up and gave us a helpless shrug.

Tic-tic, then again tic-tic. Pablo raised his hand as if he was to about to give her a reassuring wave that said 'no problem'. Instead, at the very last moment, he laid it on the horn – and held it there. He didn't look angry, he didn't say a word, just kept staring ahead, his hand pressing down hard. The seconds slipped away as the horn blared out full-force. Finally, the woman and her small dog scrambled on to the pavement.

He removed his hand, the horn stopped. The car started forward.

A few minutes later we drew up and parked on a stretch of tarmac marked PRIVADO. Having got out, we took our luggage from the boot and followed Pablo across the street in the direction of music that got louder with every step. We went through an archway into a vast enclosed courtyard where we were greeted by a multi-coloured rash of festive red, green, yellow and blue letters, three metres high, screaming from the roof: HOLIDAY VILLAGE APARTMENTS. They flashed on and off.

'Garden.' Pablo pointed, uttering his first words in nearly an hour.

Ahead, totally enclosed by tier upon tier of balconies rising up to six storeys, was a public area about the size of a football pitch, with trees, cement benches, cement paths and a swimming pool shaped like an egg timer, with an open-air bar and restaurant at its narrowest point. British paleness through to holiday reds and browns sprawled on plastic loungers; children splashed and shrieked in a paddling pool. Holiday-techno thudded out from speakers set in the palm trees.

Just inside the entrance was a large multi-language hand-printed notice. The English-language translation read:

NO DOGS. NO JOGGING. NO JUMP IN POOL.
NO BALL GAMES ONLY TABLE TENNIS, CRAZY GOLF.
NO LITTER.

Pablo pointed towards a dark and distant corner of the complex: 'Apartment. Welcome.'

After he and I had carried in the bags, we came outside again to stand for a moment in the small cordoned-off patio in front of their flat.

'Here, sometime we sit and eat. When we eat and watch them, it is like cabaret. And free.' He was pointing to the dozens of holiday apartment guests who were playing table tennis, crazy golf, drinking at the open-air bar, splashing in the cool blue waters of the swimming pool.

Yes, the swimming pool – that was the place to be. I had my trunks; all I needed was a towel. Maybe Thérèse's father fancied a swim too? I turned to ask him.

But he'd gone. One minute Pablo had been beside me, the two of us male-bonding in silent communion, and the next I was watching him push a wheelbarrow down the main path. Maybe we'd bonded and I'd missed it?

I went back indoors. The flat was on two floors: the ground floor was entirely open-plan, with zones for the kitchen, the dining room and the sitting room marked off with different coloured flooring to let you know where you were. An upwardly flowing cascade of metal steps, held together by steel tubes, led to the first-floor bathroom and bedrooms.

'Here is our home. Welcome, Jack.' Claudine was coming down the open staircase. 'Thérèse come soon. She is showering and dressing.'

Was this a hint? I'd shaved in Paris and donned my holiday best for the trip south but thanks to the Spanish heat I was already sweat-sodden and curling at the edges.

'Yes, shower and change. Great idea.'

I carried the rest of our baggage upstairs. I'd swim later.

As I was drying myself off, I happened to glance out of the bathroom window. Pablo was bent almost double over a small rockery. He straightened up for a moment, leant forward and then, with unexpected delicacy, brushed some dirt from the petals of the flower he'd just planted. Several seconds later he turned and wheelbarrowed himself off along the path and out of sight. A glimpse of life on Planet Pablo.

Coming downstairs, I heard Thérèse and Claudine below me, chatting in the kitchen zone. Immediately I realised what they were talking about I paused, my hand resting on the steel-tube banister, and I listened. They were talking in French.

'Marc was a real shit right to very end. Still, Thérèse, I'm glad you were able to go to his funeral.'

'Well – he was my father.'

'More's the pity. Aunt Lise wrote that he'd been out of town when it happened. Not changed a bit by the sound of things, the bastard. She'd heard that the no-good had been up at his lair in the mountains with some young— '

'Let's leave it, *Maman*.'

I'd been hoping to learn a bit more, but it looked like the conversation was over. At once, I continued down the rest of the stairs and went across the living-room zone to the kitchen table – shiny pine with matching pine benches – where the two women were having coffee. Thérèse, who had changed into holiday wear – a VIVA CATALUNYA! T-shirt and denim shorts – stood up and kissed me. I grinned my hello, feeling embarrassed at being kissed in front of her mother.

Claudine laughed. 'We have a shy Scottish man!'

For several seconds we sat at ease, smiling happily at each other. It was a good moment. Claudine made a remark about my correcting her English again.

'Here it is all Eurospeak: Spanish, French, English, German, Swedish, everything.'

From outside came the sound of a whistle being blown and then Pablo's voice telling someone not to jump into the pool. We couldn't help glancing towards the window and watched in silence as a line of small boys in massive shorts splashed in en masse.

'Pablo work too much. Some litter bins he buys with his own money.'

Pablo was blowing his whistle again. Another telling off. Another few seconds' silence. The three of us sat not looking at each other.

It was well before midnight when, after a late dinner, we said goodnight and went upstairs. We were travel exhausted and family-visit exhausted. As we lay in bed, I found myself thinking again about what the French policeman had told me about M. Bertrand perhaps being Thérèse's father. From the conversation I'd overheard earlier, it seemed quite possible – but how was I to bring up the topic?

Thérèse, the man you were up in the mountains with…?

Or else, a little worse: *Thérèse, I heard your mother mention something about your dad. She seemed a bit angry…*

Or worst of all: *Thérèse, I was wondering – when did you last see your father?*

By the time I was ready to speak, she was asleep.

6

Our second day began with a holiday lie-down after breakfast. Or would have done if Claudine hadn't barged into our room without knocking.

She was really embarrassed. 'So sorry, I forget.' Then she turned and vanished down the corridor.

Thérèse glared at the empty doorway. 'You see, Jack? She walk in like we are not here.' Then she jumped to her feet and shouted after her mother: 'Like she never want me to be here! Well, I fucking am here! I fucking am here!'

She slumped back down to sit on the edge of the bed. She was biting her lips and trying not to cry.

I put my arm round her and weighed in with some well-meant, heavy-duty sympathy. 'Don't worry, Thérèse. Don't take it to heart.' I reached for her hand, then continued plodding sympathetically on. So her mother forgot to knock before coming in and hadn't stuck around long enough to apologise properly, I began. A bit shocked, maybe, at seeing us near enough *in flagrante*. So no big deal. Our own fault, really. We should have locked the door. End of story.

But from Thérèse – not a word. Nothing.

I gave her hand a squeeze. After several seconds my squeeze was returned, but only faintly – out of politeness almost, it felt like. She hardly seemed aware of me, but was staring at a point far in the distance or else, even further, at somewhere deep inside her. A tear had started running down her cheek, then a second, a third.

She wiped them away, then sniffed. 'I'm going to have a bath.' She squeezed my hand again. 'I'll be all right.' She tried to give me a smile. 'Who needs parents, eh?'

Having gathered her toilet bag and a towel, she went off to the bathroom. 'See you later.'

Not knowing what to do next, I walked over to the window and stared out. Our room looked on to the street: a line of palm trees, a line of tourist coaches – one of which must have just arrived as passengers were clambering off it and stretching their legs. I watched two men head straight off the bus and into a bar directly opposite. Fast-tracking themselves into the holiday mood. Some kids were shouting they wanted to go to the beach – now! Maybe I should have a look round for a map to check out Buena Suerte, the village nearest to the wilderness part we were supposed to be visiting? Or go for a walk? A swim in the pool? The beach? The bar?

Just then there was a light knock at the bedroom door.

It was Claudine. She had come to apologise for her being 'not so polite'.

We stood in the doorway and I gave her the 'No problem, it was our own fault' routine.

She glanced into the room. 'Where is Thérèse?'

'Having a bath.'

After a few seconds' pause, Claudine cleared her throat. She seemed nervous. 'Jack?'

I nodded.

Then she asked if I would like to see some photographs of Thérèse taken when she was a little girl.

As Claudine and I sat down on the couch in the living-room zone – a couch that was also pine, with soft cushions – there was the clatter of something large, mechanical and noisy passing outside.

'Poor Pablo.' Claudine glanced over to the window. 'Today a letter from Danish man. For shouting and whistle blow at his children.' She shook her head. 'Too hard work.' Then she added: 'Some coffee?'

'No, thanks.' Then, seeing such a look of rejection pass across her face, I gave a slight cough as though to cover what

I'd just said. 'I mean, yes, please. That would be great. Thank you, Claudine.'

She beamed back at me.

Five minutes later we were sitting with a photograph album open in front of us. Coffee and biscuits were laid out within reach on a small table.

'A pretty girl.' Claudine was pointing to a blur of dark hair and ribbons that gazed out at me from between the brightly painted red bars of a playpen; across the page, a three-year-old birthday girl was bending forward to blow out candles on a cake. The eyes were Thérèse's, concentrated on the task at hand. The nearest flame was out, the second and third were still burning, almost flattened by her breath. The cake had icing on it, and writing which I couldn't read. Her small hands rested on the edge of the table to support her.

Without looking away from the photograph, Claudine said: 'Not with Pablo then, you know?' She continued: 'Thérèse tell you?'

'Oh, yes.'

'Marc was real bastard. Pablo save me, bring me here. Marc dead now, and all France is dead too for me. Pablo works. Loves Thérèse. All things I did, I did for her.'

She turned the page and pointed to a new photograph: 'See her. So brave, *la petite*.' A smile. 'This when we leave France.'

And there were the dark, dark eyes again with their familiar expression of hurt and defiance. It must have been winter; a very young Thérèse was buttoned up to the neck in a red coat complete with gloves and scarf, and she wore a bright pink knitted beret.

'Is very terrible, that hat.'

I continued to look at the eyes and the tightly clenched fists: one holding a tiny suitcase, the other a plastic bag from Monoprix. Behind her was a green train marked *Paris – Sud*. It was obvious that the small girl saw nothing of this; she was aware only of holding on to the handles of her bag and her suitcase, and staring ahead at whoever was taking the picture. Would it have been Pablo peering through the lens, checking she was in focus and looking as happy as could be hoped for in the circumstances? Meanwhile, Claudine was probably minding the luggage, glancing at her watch and thinking only of the momentous journey ahead while trying to make her daughter smile. Thérèse was supposed to be smiling – it was the beginning of their new life together, after all. An adventure.

Good for Thérèse and her sullen integrity – she won, at least on film.

A quick jerk, and the page has been turned. Snap follows snap: the arrival in Spain, the newly opened Holiday Village Apartments, their flat, Thérèse going to school, Thérèse playing in the swimming pool, Thérèse on the beach. More snaps being turned over, quicker, quicker...

Then, all at once and so suddenly I can hardly believe what I'm seeing, we've come to Thérèse when she's much older – and wearing nothing, absolutely nothing, but an embarrassed smile. She's sitting on a carpet, completely naked, a full-breasted, pubic-triangled full-frontal... Only, wait a minute, it's not Thérèse.

A closer look...

'*Merde!*' Claudine slammed the book shut. 'I am sorry, Jack.'

'It's nothing. I never saw – it was nothing.'

She stood up, clutching the album tightly in her arms. 'Yes, you saw. Please, Jack. You tell no one. It is many years long ago... when I am young, and Pablo he likes photo-making...'

'Yes, of course.' I started busying myself, rubbing away at a knot in the pine armrest as if trying to make it disappear. Then I got to my feet.

But she was already walking off. A few steps and she was more than halfway across the living-room zone. Without turning round to face me, she called back: 'I forget, and please you forget.'

'Of course, Claudine. And thanks for letting me see...'

Now she was halfway up the stairs.

'... the photographs.'

There was the sound of her bedroom door closing. The visit was not going well.

7

Lunch was awkward. From the moment Thérèse and I sat down on the bench at our side of the table, Claudine tried her hardest to be pleasant. She talked about the weather, the beach, the tourists, the crazy golf, the swimming pool. She mentioned showing me the photographs. I added they were very good photographs. Thérèse said nothing.

Claudine then suggested we go out for a meal that evening, all four of us together.

'Go where?' came from Pablo.

'Many restaurants here.' Claudine's voice was too bright.

'Too many sometimes, it seems,' she gave an exaggerated laugh.

Thérèse looked up and said something in French, but too rapidly for me to catch. Her mother looked flustered. The two women faced each other in silence. Pablo and I looked on, neither of us understanding what was happening.

Claudine spoke: 'Thérèse, I say to Jack that I am sorry for what I do.'

'And now you say to me?'

'*Mais oui*. Of course I say to you too I am sorry, Thérèse. I do not do this again – not knock and come into your room. Not again.'

For the first time since this morning Thérèse seemed to relax. 'OK, *Maman*. It's OK.'

'I know you are very angry this morning... what you say then. Of course I want you here.' Claudine seemed about to reach over to take her daughter's hand, but then didn't. She looked very unsure.

'OK, *Maman*. We forget it.' Thérèse smiled.

'Yes, that is best. That is how it is. You are away and I forget. Every day I go into room to open window for air. Today, this morning, you are here... and I forget.'

There is a moment's silence as Thérèse's smile disappears.

'You forget? I am not here for two years... then I come last night and in the morning already you forget. You *forget* I am here?'

'No, no, Thérèse.'

'It is why you are late at the station – you also forget?'

'No, no, Thérèse. No, *chérie*, please...'

'Forget, forget. Everything's forget – eh?' She stood up. 'Me and my life? Everything?' And she went rushing across the open-plan and up the staircase.

For a moment it looked as if Claudine was going to rush after her. But, having stood up, she sat down again. Pablo slid along the bench and put his arm round her shoulders.

I was about to go after Thérèse when Pablo caught my eye. 'You want to speak something?'

'Well... Well, I know that Thérèse— '

'*Sí*, our daughter Thérèse.'

'Yes, your daughter. I know that she feels very— '

'She feels, she tell us. She come to us, she tell us.'

Then he leaned over the table and jabbed his finger right in my face: 'WHO ARE YOU?'

I paused. 'What? I am... I am Jack... You know who I am. I am— '

'Please, Jack.' Claudine had started to sob. 'You go to her now. Please, you go. Yes?'

I entered our room to find Thérèse sitting on the floor with her head resting on her knees and her back to the wall. The on–off/on–off neon lighting coming from the bar opposite cast red and green stripes across the ceiling and the far wall. In the strong sunlight their reflection was weak and watery-looking against the whiteness.

I went over to her. She didn't look up.

'Thérèse, your mother was really only trying to— '

'No talk. Please, Jack, no talk.'

'But, Thérèse – she loves you. She only wants to— '

'No talk, Jack. No. No, no, no...'

Hardly above a whisper, she kept repeating the word 'no' over and over to herself. Around us, the red and green flickered on and off, then on again. I sat down beside her and held her.

8

Later that afternoon we decided to go for a swim. Maybe the world would look a better place afterwards. Sun cream and our towels from the bathroom, swimming costumes, sunglasses, a couple of paperbacks and we were ready. We clattered down the metal staircase in our sandals. No one downstairs. The entire apartment seemed empty; the lunch things had been cleared away. We didn't hang about but slipped quickly out the door and crossed the courtyard, keeping a wary lookout in case we saw Pablo. Not a sign. Out under the archway and off down the street towards the beach.

Three and a half hours of sheer pleasure. Splashing and giggling, lying in the sun. More splashing and more giggling. More lying in the sun. A drink in the bar. The holiday had started.

*

Hand in hand we strolled back – to find them both in the kitchen. Having hung up our wet towels and costumes on a drying frame just inside the front door, we came to a stop at the edge of the kitchen zone. Claudine was standing at the sink. Pablo sat at the table. From there he inspected Thérèse and me as if we were shrubs needing to be pruned or pulled out and he'd not decided which.

Claudine offered us a glass of rosé. We accepted. We sat down on our side of the pine table.

How was the beach? The beach was fine.

The water? Nice and warm.

The wine was poured. We toasted 'Salud, santé, cheers.' We sipped.

Was the beach busy? Yes, lots of people. Some British people. I mentioned the two men I'd watched getting off the bus and heading straight into the bar. Probably Scottish, I joked.

There was a pause.

Claudine took a sip of her rosé. Then a second sip. 'This afternoon Pablo and I talk about the things you say. Please, Thérèse, they are not true and very horrible.' Then she switched to French. 'Can't you understand, Thérèse? Of course I want you here. You are my only daughter, my only child. I have always wanted you. If I hadn't wanted you, I would have had you adopted.'

'Regret you didn't?'

'No, never. Marc was a bastard – we were better off without him, the two of us. I looked after you, we looked after each other.'

'Oh, yes? I was only a baby, remember?'

'It's you who can't remember, Thérèse. I worked and rushed home; I couldn't wait to be with you again— '

'Until Pablo appeared.'

'No, I loved you— '

'Past tense.'

'You're twisting things, Thérèse. I loved you. I still love you.'

'Is that why you barged into my room this morning, as if I wasn't there? As if you wanted me not to be there? Like always.'

'Not always. Not ever, Thérèse. Anyway, the past is over and done with. Finished. Pablo and I never talk about it. There's no point. Now that Marc's dead… '

'My father— '

'You hardly knew him, Thérèse. You were a child.'

'Not when I went back to France.'

'But you never saw him then.'

'Didn't I?'

'You never said.'

'No, I never said.'

Claudine looked baffled. 'So, what are you saying now?'

'He was *my* father. My real father. We met for lunch once. We met for dinner. He gave me presents. He gave me this.' She held up the silver pendant, then, when Claudine leaned forward to look more closely, let it fall back.

'But Marc never wrote. He would have written to say he'd met you.'

'He never knew.'

There was a long pause, as if Thérèse had let a stone fall down into a deep well and we were all waiting to hear it strike something.

Claudine was the first to speak. 'What do you mean, "he never knew"?'

Thérèse shrugged, then turned away to stare out of the window.

'Thérèse? Who did you tell him you were?'

'Nobody special.'

'Who did he think you were?'

93

Without turning her head Thérèse replied: 'Probably he didn't think anything. I was a young girl; he liked young girls. He liked me. Some people do.'

'But... but if you didn't tell him who you were... What were you hoping for?'

She wheeled round. 'My father, of course. My *real* father.' She glanced at Pablo. 'Is that so difficult to understand?'

Pablo strained forward as if to interrupt.

Thérèse beat him to it. 'You just keep the fuck out of this.' Then she glared back at her mother. 'When Pablo brought us here I lost my friends, my language, my country. Only seven years old and I'd lost MY WHOLE FUCKING LIFE!' she screamed at them. 'Of course I wanted my father!'

After a pause, Claudine spoke: 'Thérèse, I don't understand. Do you mean that – that you – that you and he— ?'

'*Did she?* That's what you're wondering now, isn't it? With her own father? *Did she?*'

Claudine looked too confused to reply. Pablo's eye had started a slow and furious tic-tic-tic. Eventually he spoke: 'You, girl – you are bad. Bad!'

Thérèse was walking very quickly. I had to nearly double-step to keep up with her. Once we got beyond the din of the courtyard and outside into the street, I asked her: 'So, M. Bertrand at the mountains, he really was your father?'

She didn't break stride: '*Mais oui.*'

There didn't seem anything else to say. We continued walking.

We spent the rest of the evening drifting round the town, wandering up and down the beach. A few late-night gift shops, a few noisy bars. Dinner was mostly wine, tears and silence. It was well after midnight when we returned to the Holiday Village Apartments. The night air was hot, breathless and heavy. There was no music. The poolside was deserted, the water utterly still. The flat was in darkness.

We found their note pinned to the cork message-board. Thérèse read it out, crumpled it into a ball and threw it on the tiles. She started kicking it round the floor.

'They go on holiday for three days (kick). To let things calm (kick). PS: We will please feel at home!' (one final mega-kick that sent her staggering).

She landed up next to the drinks cabinet and took out the whisky we'd brought as a present. It hadn't even been opened.

'Santé! To wilderness life!' She drank from the bottle, wrinkling her nose. 'Not favourite to drink. Sorry, Jack.'

She lurched across the room. Raising her arm up high, she poured the rest of it, nearly an entire litre of the best single malt, down the sink.

'This is our fucking PS.' She slammed the empty bottle on to the draining board.

Then she leaned over the sink. 'Don't feel good.'

Next morning we set off for the wilderness.

September 2003

1

Next day: the train back to Barcelona, change stations. Into the sun, then into another train. Rattling up into the hills towards the town of Vic. Out of the train and into the sun again. An hour later, climbing into a bus. Rattling out into the countryside. Getting hotter and hotter. The door opening to let passengers on or off – a brief, cooling draught, then the door closing again. The bus becoming even hotter than before.

'What?'

I leaned across the aisle to hear what Thérèse had just said. She was pointing out of the window.

'Look!'

I stared. I could see a lake. The surface of the water was quite motionless, shimmering in the heat as if the scene it reflected had been cut on to a sheet of molten steel.

Then suddenly I saw what she meant.

What I'd taken for a cloud's shadow on the lake – not that there were any clouds, of course, nor much water for a lake – was really a sunken church. Steeple and roof rose straight up into the sunlight and, like some vast water beast, it had a line of birds perched along its tiled spine. Gaps for windows showed along the dark stone wall, and the upper part of the main door was exposed. Clearly the dam should have been much fuller. The sides seemed to be holding little more than a scooped-out emptiness with a puddle at the bottom.

'Reservoir – they drowned the old village. When they can see the church, water is very low. Not good. But we are nearly arrived.'

It was late afternoon.

A cloud of red dust, red earth, a few shuttered houses, a shop, a garage with a single petrol pump – that was my first sight of Buena Suerte. The dust stuck to the sweat on our skin and the heat stuck to the dust, so we breathed in heat, dust and sweat. Having dropped us, the bus swept round to face the way it had come and blue-farted itself out of the village. Back to the real world.

I watched the bus disappear with the sense that the road was disappearing with it. A heat haze rose from a dried-up river bed that was a tumbled bank of rocks, stunted-looking cactus plants, old fridges, rusted tins and plastic bags. On what might have once been a river bank was a scattering of skeletons that might once have been trees, stick-thin and colourless except for the occasional drab patch of brown-green leaves. A small brown lizard stopped itself in mid-dart along the low stone wall at the side of the road. Quite motionless apart from its heartbeat, it gazed at me for several seconds. With a flick of its tail, it was gone. A fig tree hung over the wall; a purplish mash of figs lay trodden into the dirt at my feet. *Gach-gach* – a bird screeched somewhere above me. It was hot-hot-hot. I felt dirty and thirsty.

'It's a fucking oven.'

'Toni say we look for the shop and ask for Jésus. He is the owner.' Thérèse shouldered her rucksack and walked off.

Ask for Jésus. I was too dirty, thirsty and tired even to make the obvious joke. Every time I licked my lips I got another tongue's worth of dust into my mouth; the rest of me was sweaty hair, sweaty skin, sweaty T-shirt, sweaty jeans and grime. Mostly grime.

That's when I realised we were being watched. Now the red dust had settled, I could see a shop-front up ahead. It had an overhanging roof for shade, and under this veranda were a few men, some standing, some squatting. They gazed out at us intently. Not friendly, not unfriendly – just gazing. In total silence. One of them was rolling a cigarette. Never taking his eyes off us, he rolled the paper back and forth between his fingers.

Once he held the cigarette between his lips, he made no attempt to light up but let his hands fall to his sides.

Thérèse had stopped about a metre short of the veranda rail. There was no sign of anyone standing aside to let her through.

 It might be rural Spain, but as far as I was concerned this was familiar territory. For the blue sky, the heat, the dust road and the silent Spaniards read: low cloud, rain, the main street and a bunch of locals in small-town central Scotland. The paths of two Scotsmen, complete strangers, cross and they'll greet each other with a nod-and-grunt that's halfway between a choked breath and a strangled 'Aye'. There's no smile, no invitation to further conversation; the nod-and-grunt says it all: *Here we are, the two of us, in this fucking place, right enough; and there's fuck all to be done about it.*

I stepped past Thérèse and went up on to the veranda, giving my best half-nod, half-grunt all round, hoping to take in everyone at once. As I reached for the handle, a very tall man wearing a denim boiler suit nodded to me and smiled. '*Buenos días.*' He stood aside to let us enter.

'*Buenos días.*' I went into the shop. Thérèse followed.

Tins, plastic bags, cardboard boxes, more tins. Shelves of tins, boxes of tins – but at least it was cooler than outside. We asked for Jésus, and he appeared. A shy man, with no English. Thérèse and he discussed what was wanted: a three-litre wine box as a present; Thérèse stocked up on extra soap and toothpaste. A few minutes later, the door swung open and a man entered the shop. He paused before stepping forward; his outline stood clear in the doorway against the fierce sunlight outside. He looked to be in his mid-thirties – a warm smile, an untrimmed beard, black hair, bright eyes. There was a cry of greeting.

'*Cómo estás*, Thérèse?'

'Toni!'

He embraced her, kissing her on each cheek. The two of us were introduced. This was her friend Toni – we'd be staying with him and Charlie – and I was her friend. 'Very good friend,' she added. I made to shake hands, but Toni embraced me too.

'Thérèse my good friend – you my good friend.'

The three of us came out on to the porch, a nod to everyone there, then we stepped down into the street. In our absence, the sunlight had been sharpened for our return, its touch like the slash of an open knife.

2

Who'd want a Ferrari when you could sit on the back of a Toyota pick-up complete with swollen-looking, rough-country tyres? Who cared about the heat, so long as you made sure not to touch the metal bodywork when climbing in? It was miles of pure heaven: blue sky above, a rush of deliciously warm air around us and the occasional lurch or bump underneath. Whether it was the relief at finally getting away from her family or else at having at last said something about what had happened with her father, Thérèse looked genuinely at ease for once, leaning against the back of the cab, legs stretched out, hair blown about her face. At first we shouted to each other over the roar of the engine, pointing out the different sorts of cactus, the intricate layout of low stone walls between fields, the occasional picture-postcard Spanish farmhouse with its courtyard, stone horse trough and curving wrought-iron balconies, its windowsills spilling over with red and yellow flowers. Every so often, brightly coloured birds swooped down near us, and twice we saw a bird of prey motionless in the empty sky.

The further we travelled, the more frequent became the lurches and bumps. Then the pick-up splashed its way across a shallow ford marked by a pair of rusty oil drums on the 'civilised' side and a pair of trees on the other, where the wilderness proper began. The water never rose higher than the hubcaps, and a cooling dampness settled over us as we crossed. It was a wide stretch of river, the current slack and the surface mirror-still apart from the blunted V-shaped trail of ripples we drew after us fanning out on either side. Once clear of the water, we climbed a low hill, the Toyota skidding and slipping on the loose stones.

Half an hour later we stopped. In front of us was a house set thirty metres or so back from the road, with the curtains pulled and the door shut. It looked like a single-storey wooden box raised almost a metre off the ground; it was painted green in some parts, overpainted brown in others, and had an olive-green tarpaulin roof. The garden, its wooden gate propped half-open, was a straggle of vegetable patches, strips of black plastic held down by old tyres, rolls of chicken wire, weeds and dirt. A rusted yellow van stood in the far corner.

When Toni sounded the horn, a few hens clucked and flapped themselves briefly into the air and a ragged cockerel fluttered up on to a nearby tyre. Taking a good grip of the rubber, it gave us the Hard Stare, one eye at a time. That aside, nothing happened. After another blast of the horn, one of the curtains was pulled aside, a hand waved.

Toni climbed out of the cab, placed a cardboard box just inside the gate and yelled: '*Ciao*, Dolores!'

Seconds later we were again bumping and lurching down the trail at not much more than walking pace; we were jerked from side to side, our hands holding on as best they could. The dirt track was getting worse with every metre: when it divided a couple of hundred metres further on, Toni leaned out of his window and pointed down the narrower fork, to the left. 'This way go to Marshall's place. Our neighbour.' He slapped the roof of the cabin. 'This his pick-up. Our place next.'

Ten minutes later the engine was cut and all we could hear was birdsong and the rasp of insects. Toni's shack stood to our left, a few metres down a slope of sandy-coloured earth, dried-out bushes and cacti, which dropped away for half a kilometre or so towards a tree-lined gully. Here and there, fig and almond trees shed patches of shade. A cloudless blue sky stretched above. After only a few seconds the heat had started to grip and squeeze the sweat out of us.

We clambered off the Toyota. The sweat was now in my eyes, running down my face, my chest, my back. Around us, everything shimmered; the very colours seemed to have been scorched away, fading into a blanched emptiness until, far in the distance, the line of mountains rose up, blue-black.

The shack was a single room nailed together from recycled wooden pallets, chipboard, corrugated iron, plastic sheeting and timber. With its outdoor kitchen-cum-sitting room courtyard partly covered by a tarpaulin canopy, it looked more like a piece of sculpture set in an open-air gallery of purest sunlight than a house. We were shown where the mobile phone was kept – strictly for emergencies only – on the shelf above their mattress. It had hardly been used in the last five years, we were assured – only twice, and both times to tell Jésus to be sure Charlie brought back matches when she was in getting the supplies. There was no TV, no radio even. The food was kept in a large tin box, so it didn't get shared with the local wildlife.

There was no electricity and no plumbing – water had to be carried up from the river in pails and canvas water-bags. Last thing at night the bed had to be checked for wrigglies; first thing in the morning clothes and shoes had to be turned upside down and shaken. Oh, and we should watch out for vipers – whenever we went walking through long grass, we had to be sure to stamp the ground to keep them away. Near the river there were water snakes – these, we were told, were very gentle. A whip snake, nearly two metres long, lived in the woodpile. It was so shy that we wouldn't even know it was there. The simple life.

We were very tired. The rest of that first day remains as fragments, a series of snapshots:

Charlie as an upward flow of streaming red hair and purple underskirt coming towards us through the long grass. She's shouting a welcome. She and Thérèse embrace. We are introduced.

Thérèse and I are pitching our tent some thirty metres or so from the house near one of the fig trees. Its branches are heavy with purple fruit. I pick one and bite into its wet, ripe sweetness. 'Paradise, or what?' I say to Thérèse. The ground is littered with fallen fruit, some dried out like shrunken scrotums, others split generously open.

Darkness in a couple of hours: I'm down on my knees at the back of the tent, the continuous rasp and buzz of insects is like another wall around me. Leaning forward, I hammer in the final tent peg, my face pressed full into the clogged nylon smell of the material until I'm almost choking. Breathless for a moment, I have to stop, lean back into the insect noise (a harsh, grating sound, strangely familiar, though I can't quite place it) and feel the vastness of the countryside stretching into the distance. A few seconds later I have recovered enough to fix the tent loop over the peg and tap it down.

Our skinny-dip coolness from a lively splash-about in the river has turned to sweat again by the time we've climbed back up the slope to the shack. Five minutes under the shower. Always a shared experience as someone has to be on hand to refill the sieve-like canvas bucket rigged up to hang at just above head height. While darkness gathers at the edge of the yard, we take turns at being the shower-filler and the showered-upon. Glancing across the courtyard, I see Charlie standing next to an ancient gas cooker, unconnected of course: she's adding vegetables to a pot while Toni crouches down beside her, level with the grill compartment. There's a bundle of twigs under where the gas jets would have been, and he's puffing himself red in the face to bring the cooking fire into flame.

It's quite dark, and much cooler. We're sitting under the open-air tarpaulin veranda between the snake-house woodpile and the shack. Charlie lights a mosquito coil and blows at the end to make it glow. A moment later, a thread of greyish smoke rises – an acrid sweetness.

Tonight we are served meal number one: seasonal veg on a bed of lentils. (Number two is seasonal veg on a bed of rice; number three, a bed of pasta. On our fourth night it's back to number one again.) As guests of honour, Thérèse and I have been placed in the leather-cushioned comfort of two old car seats; Charlie, stretched at her ease on a wooden deckchair as if she were on an ocean liner and travelling first class, is picking out what had once been a tune on what had once been a guitar; Toni is a pasha, seated on a heap of folded-up sacks and pieces of carpet, leaning back against the woodpile.

'Yeuch!' Thérèse gives a little-girl screech. 'Yeuch! Yeuch! Yeuch!'

Charlie passes over a spoon: 'Here, Thérèse. Just fish them out.' Then she smiles at me. 'Sorry, I should have warned you guys. Best to cover your cup when you're not actually drinking.'

I look down and see a thrashing mass of small legs and wings as half a dozen biters and scratchers peg out their last in my after-dinner coffee. Are their tiny lives passing in front of their eyes? More to the point, do things that small shit themselves? I scoop them out and hope for the best. The paraffin lamp burns from the overhanging roof; despite the smouldering coil, the surrounding darkness is an agitation of moths, mosquitoes and other biters whose shadows cluster around us without ever settling. I look up into the night sky and see a falling star.

Once we have eaten, Toni tells us about their nearest neighbours, Marshall and Rosa, the couple who work the place whose road-end we passed on the way in.

'Marshall is American, from "the good ole USA". Today I meet him where we swim in river, and he tell me Bush ask Congress for a hundred billion dollars to bomb Iraq. He ask, and he get. Marshall hate Bush. He hate Disney and McDonald's. He is very angry man, and very mad. He has plan. He build the future, and call it Paradise. At first he and Rosa work all day until near dead. They hammer, they dig, they scream loud to each other. Now only Marshall work. Rosa sit and do nothing. She say she wait for Paradise.'

Being the perfect host, he's rolling a joint to celebrate our arrival and has reached the tricky stage of tight-twisting the end.

'Not me and Charlie,' he goes on. 'Dig toilet, build shack. Relax – and live! *Tranquil*, eh? Not Señor Marshall! Many fence-post to make Paradise: three hundred and thirty-seven fence-post. His bit of Spain. His bit of madness.'

The joint is ready now. He lights it, and by the flaring match there's his deeply tanned face, his black curly beard and easy smile. After a deep draw he passes it over to Charlie. Then it's our turn.

Toni continues: we must go and see Marshall's place. And check out the man's eyes!

Three joints later the flow of time slows down to a complete stop. Thérèse has risen to full stretch on her toes, bringing her hands together to kill a mosquito: she holds the position forever and, silhouetted in starlight, looks more graceful than any dancer.

Nearly dawn. The faintest pale light is seeping into the tent.

'Jack? You awake, Jack?'

Not any longer. Sounding as sleepy as I can, I reply: 'No.'

'Don't open your eyes. Stay still.'

She's slid closer, put her arm round me on the outside of my sleeping-bag; the side of her face up against mine, she whispers into my ear: 'We are together again. Like we were in Paris but better, *non*? We forget my mother, we forget Pablo. Now is just you and me.'

'No Pablo, no Claudine – sounds fine.' I must still be half-asleep because I hear myself adding a moment later: 'But... your father?'

She sits up abruptly. 'Please, Jack, you understand – my father not know.' She settles beside me again. 'Last time he saw me I was two years old. Younger, maybe. A baby. When we meet I tell him I am Thérèse Galvez – I not want to lose him again. It is my true name – *Maman* change our name when we come to Spain with Pablo. My father not know... anything.'

I lie tense, my fists clenched inside my sleeping-bag. I remember the penthouse, the icy wind, the armfuls of brightly coloured clothes she heaped on to her father's body. Her rushing out into the snowstorm. She's on her knees, her hands clawing at the snow. She's screaming, she's weeping...

'Jack?'

'Yes?'

'I will not lose *you*?'

The light from outside is getting stronger by the second; abruptly, from a nearby tree, a bird starts on its morning scales. Another answers it. Then a third.

'Jack?'

'It's all right, Thérèse. Everything's fine.'

'You hold me? Talk to me?'

'Everything's fine, Thérèse.' My eyes are shut against the gathering light coming through the tent wall. Suddenly I feel utterly worn out, completely drained.

'Please, Jack.'

Though my whole body feels leaden-heavy and exhausted, I force myself to turn round and hold her. Soon it gets uncomfortably warm lying so close together in our sleeping-bags, but I keep holding her.

I stroke her hair. I whisper her name a few times. I repeat that everything's fine.

3

The after-breakfast heat was like a blow to the face when we stepped out from under the tarpaulin covering next to the shack; the insect noise was already set at full volume. Sunlight glared back at us, its harshness becoming an unsteady haze only with distance and giving the trees across the valley a slowed-down underwater look.

We took a second step, and the insect noise was abruptly switched off. There was a sudden tension, an urgency we could feel surrounding us as if the whole valley was holding its breath. No clouds, no jet trails, the empty sky arranged round a point of solitary stillness: an eagle, perhaps, pinned invisibly into position high above us. A few more steps, and the insect clamour had once more relaxed to that familiar-sounding rasp up and down its single-note scale.

Toni gave us some wisdom-of-the-wilderness advice before we left: 'Remember: in long grass, stamp hard to scare snakes.'

We nodded.

'River water good for drink.'

Nod number two. I joked: *a label each round our necks?* No, this was no joking matter, Toni insisted; it was real wilderness we were heading into: once off the main trail there'd be no paths, no signposts, only a free-for-all among the wild horses, lizards, snakes and scorpions. We promised to be back in time for lunch.

The track began just beyond the discreetly screened latrine-hole where I'd squatted after breakfast: a quick squat and out, with no lingering. We were to follow the wheel ruts of broken stones for a half-kilometre or so, to where the track split: our path would be the one going down to the right. We began walking, and sweating.

Thérèse didn't speak. Two days at her parents and she'd become a stranger all over again: eighteen years old, rainbow hair, olive skin, a fondness for silver jewellery and secrecy.

A quarter of an hour later, having come through a small wood crammed with the chatter and rush of birds, we collided with the sun again. Sweat started running from every pore, and the flies stuck to our skin.

'Why big rush? *Sont les vacances, non?*' Thérèse was calling to me from a few metres away, still keeping to the edge of the wood for shade.

Meanwhile, another few kilos melted and rolled off me. After the turn in the path, we saw, below us, a perfectly flat stretch of cleared land, about one hundred and fifty metres on each side: Marshall's place, lying like a design branded by the heat on to the baked red earth.

Not one tree, not a single bush or flower grew in that meticulously fenced-in area. There was a small wooden cabin with steps down to the open yard, a series of what looked like low-walled sheep pens, beyond lay several vegetable plots and, heaped here and there, building materials. Closer to, we could see that the sheep pens were really the walls-in-progress of a half-dozen unfinished buildings; stacked nearby, their doors and window frames had started to rot, some panes of glass were smashed, tiles and breeze blocks were broken, planks split; the various piles were tufted with grass and brightly coloured weeds. At first glance it was difficult to tell whether the site was under construction or in the process of being dismantled one breeze block at a time.

According to Toni, the man had only ever had one idea in his head: having fence-posted and barbed-wired his land, he'd measured it out to the last square centimetre and made a detailed plan of the site, everything drawn to a precise scale. All the proposed buildings were being worked on simultaneously, a day at a time, which explained why none of the walls looked much more than half a metre high.

The insect noise was louder than ever, and the brilliance of the light seemed to have sharpened the yellowed grass. We went down the slope to where the path ended in a patch of baked earth. A forty-year-old schoolboy a good few inches shorter than me and with stuck-on beard, shorts, sandals and baseball cap, glanced over at us. Instead of a satchel he wore a plastic cylinder strapped to his back. Mad-eyed Marshall, it had to be. Even before saying hello he called across to a woman sitting over by the cabin in the shade of a tattered café umbrella with a faded Martini logo. Now that we were closer I could hear faint tinny voices coming from the small radio on her lap. A moment later she switched it off and got up from her canvas picnic seat. She took a few steps towards him... then stopped. This was Rosa.

Marshall and Rosa, Jack and Thérèse. Four people standing in Paradise.

Marshall walked over and knelt at Rosa's feet. She must have been aware of our approach but gave no sign.

His first words to us were shouted: 'Lysenko. Ever hear of him?'

An American accent, all right. Two polite shakes of our heads were our only contribution to the lecture that followed. While the sun pressed down on us, wringing sweat from every pore, mad-eyed Marshall monologued about the planned farming methods devised by Comrade Lysenko for Revolutionary Russia.

The woman looked at us over the top of his head and poured chemicals into the tank on his back. In her mid-thirties or maybe older, Spanish-looking, hard-faced and with long straggly black hair, she was dressed in a T-shirt and ragged shorts. She was barefoot, her skin burned brown-black.

Tank filled and cap screwed safely back on, Marshall scrambled to his feet. We introduced ourselves and thanked him for kindly lending his Toyota to pick us up the previous day. We tried to get a good look at his eyes. Difficult, as he hardly ever glanced in our direction now that he was no longer doing the talking: instead, shifting his weight from foot to foot in frustration, he stared over at his knee-high buildings and was clearly waiting for us to leave. A small lizard held on to the side of the wall nearest us, clinging miraculously to the sun-warmed stonework; it paid us no attention.

He followed our polite enquiry about how long it would be until the building work was finished with a nod, as if agreeing to something we'd said. Then he walked straight up to Thérèse: 'Nothing out here, woman, but what really matters.'

He waited for her to make some reply.

She said nothing. When he made no move to step away, she smiled at him finally. Her first smile of the day. Then she nodded.

Marshall grinned a schoolboy grin in return, gave us a wave and trotted off, his cylinder bouncing up and down on his back.

As she turned towards us, Rosa didn't bother disguising her weariness. She offered us a drink of water from a plastic barrel that stood against the side of the cabin in the shade. Civilities observed, we left. Ever-fainter pop music coming from the radio escorted us from the property.

We cut off from the track to make our way down to the river.

'He's crazy, all right!' was my considered opinion.

'*Mais, il est…* cute,' was Thérèse's surprising response.

'Cute for a gnome, maybe; all he needs is the fishing rod.'

End of conversation.

We found a stretch where the river was slightly deeper and shaded by trees on either side, forming a natural patchwork of leaves, branches and birdsong. Lard-white Scottish flesh and nut-brown Continental nakedness stepped into the water – and at once there was an upwards scrabble of red and yellow birds fluttering between the overhanging branches of a tree. Behind us, we could see the path we'd followed from the Marshalls'; the cactus bushes and scrub we'd passed looked almost seared white in the heat. We lay down in the coolness, the water deep enough to float in. A favourite place, to judge by the knotted rope hanging from one of the trees. Far above us we knew the sun still blazed.

Just then we heard hooves. Moments later, nearly a dozen wild horses came careering down a track between the trees on the opposite bank. Seeing us, they stopped abruptly and stared over. Then they began ambling up and down the stretch of loose stones, edging ever closer to the water. Finally, standing in the river to cool down, they took turns, it seemed, to raise their heads every so often and stare at us. They weren't genuinely wild horses, we'd been told, but had been turned loose over the years, singly or in pairs, because their owners no longer wanted them. Mostly they were getting old. In time, they had banded together. Two of them were pure white, the rest piebald, blacks, greys, browns with white manes. Nomads that kept to the valley, never straying far from the river. Nervous rather than frightened, they let themselves be caught and used when required. Toni had Tombo and Evie in his field full time; they seemed happy enough.

Sometimes at night, once things had started to go very wrong, I'd leave our tent and walk down to the river to be by myself. Often I'd sit near where we'd bathed that day and listen to the water purling on the stones and to the night calls from the unseen branches above. The horses were usually somewhere near, less a noise than a sense of restlessness in the darkness.

That first afternoon, lying on my back in the water, staring up into the nearness of green and into the depth of cloudless blue beyond, and with the current trailing Thérèse's hair against my bare shoulder, I felt relaxed, soothed. So did she.

It was a truly happy moment.

4

Thanks mostly to the heat and the dope, the days were very much the same – and soon they'd all blurred into the one same day that was endlessly repeated: dawn/sunshine/fierce sunshine/coolness/darkness/then dawn again.

In the company of Toni and Charlie everything was leisurely. They got up in the morning, filled their day with more or less pleasurable moments, then went back to sleep again. Thérèse and I fitted in as best we could. There was no need for anyone to do anything they didn't want to do. We passed the time chatting, going for long walks, lazing by the river, working on the vegetable patch (courgettes, peppers, lettuce, onions, cucumbers, tomatoes); in the evening we'd smoke some dope, eat some dinner, smoke some more dope, then go to bed. It was pleasant, and it was pointless. Soon the very pointlessness itself ceased to matter.

Once a week Charlie made the two-hour drive into Vic to teach basic English at the small primary school. She would get up early, go for a swim, get dressed in the smart blouse and summer skirt she'd washed in the river after the previous week. In return for borrowing Marshall's pick-up, she collected the weekly provisions for both households. We gave her our bank cards and PIN numbers so she could withdraw our contribution to the communal expenses. That evening was always celebratory.

One night, a few weeks after we'd arrived, we had just gone to bed when I heard Thérèse sobbing next to me in the darkness.

I turned over and put my arm round her. We lay like that for several minutes, then she spoke. 'I get close to someone – I lose them. Now you, you not want make love to me. Not like before.'

'Of course I do. I'm just tired.' It was true. Every night I climbed into the sleeping-bag my body felt leaden-heavy even though I'd not been doing anything much all day. 'Very, very tired. Really.'

'You *think* you want, that is all.'

Christ, was this Analytical Anna's ghost come long-distance to haunt me?

'I love you, Thérèse.'

'Oh, yes?' There was venom in her voice. 'Tell me.'

'Well... I do, Thérèse, I really do.' What else was there to say?

The two of us lay in an angry silence. Finally, she whispered: 'Jack? Jack?' Her hand was feeling for mine in the darkness.

'Jack. I am sorry. *J'ai peur*, is all.'

'You're frightened? But – what of?'

She gripped my hand tighter, struggling to hold back her sobs. 'I am frightened I will lose again everything.'

'But there's me. You've got me.'

How perfectly masterful I felt, how very much the man giving his woman the strength and support she needed. Feeling less exhausted by the second, I put my arm round her and pulled her close to me. 'I'm here, remember. You're not going to lose me.' I let her rest safely on my manly chest, stroked her hair. 'Don't you worry,' I whispered, kissing the top of her head. How easy it all seemed.

Between sobs, she managed: 'You will look after me?'

'Of course, of course.'

'Protect me. You will take care for me?'

'Of course, of course.' My manly chest was expanding. In fact, I was waking up all over. A record-speed erection had begun pushing up the material of my sleeping-bag. And, even better, I could feel Thérèse's hand sliding down to make contact.

'You will stay always with me, not leave me?' She was rubbing up and down over the little tentlet my prick was making for itself.

'Of course.' With my free hand I started to unzip my sleeping-bag.

'Now that I lose everything, *you* will be everything for me? Yes?'

The zip was down. Her hand had moved smoothly inside to continue its good work.

I kissed her hair again. 'Yes, everything, Thérèse. I promise.'

'You will be like my best daddy? You will look after me, always?'

Her hand had made me action-man stiff, but for a split second after she'd spoken I wavered. What the hell was going on? What was this 'daddy' stuff?

Next second I was thinking: Fuck it, who cares?

'Yes, yes!' I urged while unzipping her bag.

More wide awake and bed-lively than I'd felt in a long time, I pulled aside the top of her sleeping-bag. In the very faint moon and starlight that came through the tent wall she lay as half-shadow – her lips, her shoulders, her breasts and the curve of her stomach – and as darkness: her dark hair, her eyes, the hollows under her arms, between her legs. Her nakedness was seared by the small gash of brightness on her chest, the silver pendant. And then I lost it. No sooner had I begun entering her than somewhere inside me the power was switched off. Sudden and overwhelming exhaustion. Total collapse.

I could have wept, I could have screamed. 'I'm sorry, Thérèse. I'm so sorry,' I whispered.

For her part, the moment she was free of my weight she zipped up her sleeping-bag and rolled over to lie with her back to me.

'I'm really sorry, Thérèse.'

Silence.

I lay awake for hours. Shortly before dawn I reached the only solution that seemed possible. I decided to leave. At first light I'd quietly gather up my holdall – my passport and cash were still in it – then leave. I'd get dressed outside the tent so as not to wake her. Without a word to anyone, I'd start walking back along the track to Buena Suerte. I had tried my best but, for whatever reason, I had failed. Thérèse would be better off without me. I'd be leaving her among friends.

In the course of the next few hours, I managed to convince myself that abandoning her was an honourable sacrifice on my part. Just as it had been with Anna.

5

I slept in and woke late, to find that Thérèse had beaten me to it. She had gone. Her rucksack was gone too.

I was furious.

I wrenched on my jeans, opened the flap and climbed out. Already the day's heat was like a solid wall, insect noise like another wall, and sunlight bleaching all colour out of the scrub, the nearby trees and the sky.

'*Buenos días,*' Toni called over from where he was sitting in the shade of the tarpaulin. 'Coffee?'

'Thanks,' I called back.

Coffee, then I was leaving.

By the time I'd wandered down the slope for a discreet al fresco piss, wandered back up, had a wash in the plastic bucket and slipped into yesterday's river-rinsed and moon-dried T-shirt, the coffee was made. I sat down.

'Charlie's gone to Vic. To talk English with her twenty-thirty *niños*. All day noise-noise-noise. She loves them.' He poured out the coffee. 'She'll come back after going to Jésus's shop.' He handed me a packet of biscuits. 'You like?'

'Thanks.' I took two.

We sat without speaking. I drank my coffee, ate my two biscuits. The sun got hotter, the grass and trees more colour-less.

He poured me a second cup. 'I think Thérèse go this morning, with Charlie.'

'Yes.'

'She will come back later. No worries.' He stood up. 'Today I have something that is big surprise for you. Come!'

OK, I thought to myself. I'll see his big surprise, then leave.

Toni rolled a joint and we set off. From the main track we took a turn-off so overgrown it was almost impossible to make out. This led us into a part of the valley I had never explored before; on either side the country was a straggle of scrub, occasional trees and metre-high cacti.

From time to time he pointed out things of local interest.

'Here the horses come and sometimes we catch them to ride... Here is good place for fish... Here good for rabbits... Up on the hill lives a man. Very private man; we never see. From Sweden. He speaks English very good... Today is real hot, no? Next time we go on Tombo and Evie.' In this friendly way we walked for a leisurely twenty minutes.

The abandoned farmhouse had been built partway down a slope, which gave it a view of the river below and the sweep of the valley beyond. It stood in what had once been a cobbled courtyard, now overgrown with weeds. Apart from Marshall's ongoing master plan, this was the only stone building I'd seen since arriving. It had the remains of a wooden veranda staggering round its walls, and louvre-type shutters drooped like badly hung flags in front of gaps that had once been windows. The roof had been patched in a couple of places with corrugated-iron sheeting; a few odd tiles were still in place, but most of the unprotected rafters showed through. An attractive enough place, if it hadn't been falling apart. The veranda was rotted, with most of the planks lying where they had fallen off. The front door was tied with red twine looped round the handle and attached to a nail hammered into the frame; the main panel was missing – as if the owner had forgotten his key one day and simply punched his way in.

Toni unwound the twine from round the nail. 'Old *finca*, farmhouse for all the valley. Stands in middle.' He put his shoulder to the door. 'No one has visited inside for a couple of years. No one lives here for many years. And so the house— ' the door suddenly gave ' —going to pieces.'

Inside, even the sunlight seemed discoloured and rancid, filtered through a haze of cloth that was more grime than curtain. The stove had been removed and replaced by the broken bricks, bird feathers and rubble that had come down the chimney. Where worn matting had been ripped away, the wooden floor showed through. Tattered wallpaper hung in forlorn streamers. The ceiling, for the most part, lay on the floor.

'Is *peligroso*. Take care, please – the floor has many holes. It is bad. No worries. It can be fixed.'

Can be fixed?

Our footsteps echoed in the large main room; traces of dried birdshit crusted the underside of some rafters and had spattered on to the floorboards.

There was no furniture except for the remains of a sorry-looking piano: the front panel was smashed, the keys yellowed and mostly missing, strings stuck out in the air like feelers. It stood in the centre of the room, as if it had been pushed there and abandoned. Musically, it was in worse shape than I was. Without thinking what I was doing, I let my right hand form the chord of C major, then at the last moment pressed down the more desolate C minor instead. Not that the instrument, poor thing, could express the difference. There was an uncertain rattle from the strings, a dull *clunk*, then, a good couple of seconds later, came a metallic-sounding *ping*. It spoke on behalf of the house and seemed to say it all.

Then came his big surprise.

'This will be new home for you and Thérèse. You would like? Some work, but I will help. Charlie will help too.'

As the *ping* slowly died, I could hear an insect hitting itself against the bars of the shutters, unable, it seemed, to aim with any success for the light outside. I walked over to the window. The frame was edged with jagged glass; a wisp of what looked like sheep's wool had snagged there and blew backwards and forwards in a draught I myself couldn't feel. I stared out, keeping my back to the ravaged piano. The morning after my father died, I'd carried armfuls of Mozart, Haydn and the rest out into the back green and burned the lot.

'Come, I show you best room where you can start to live,' Toni called to me.

I went through to join him in the back room. It was much darker here, and felt airless. The small window, its glass miraculously intact, was smeared opaque with filth and cobwebs and hanging with lumps of dead flies and other dried-up morsels. The slatted shutters had rusted half-open; they sliced the sunlight into thin strips of brightness that cut into the dirt and debris littering the floor.

An old mattress lay against one wall – it was grubby, stained and probably half-alive.

'This room could be good beginning home for you and Thérèse. We will clean the floor and the walls. We will get a new mattress. We fix the roof. No worries.' Toni was looking encouragingly at me. 'We work together – we make a very good house.'

Such a good, kindly, generous man.

'Yes,' I managed to reply. 'With work, maybe…'

I left the sentence unfinished. The back room of his 'big surprise' had taken away any lingering doubts I might have had about leaving.

6

But yet again Thérèse had beaten me to it. As I turned the corner of the track, heading straight to the tent, for my rucksack and escape, I saw her up ahead. She was sitting at the edge of the yard, wearing her VIVA CATALUNYA! T-shirt and shorts, and with her rucksack on the ground beside her. She watched us approach.

When we were about fifty metres from her, I waved.

No response.

I waved to her again and called 'Hello!'

Not even the slightest nod of her head in return. She remained as she was, cross-legged, hands in her lap: sitting motionless in the full sun.

Toni gave me a friendly nod of encouragement. 'Maybe I will go to check the water for Tombo and Evie, then for a swim. Good luck, Jack!' He went towards the horses' corral.

Once I'd turned off the path and was coming down the slope, I tried again: 'Hi, Thérèse!'

She stared back at me and made no reply.

A full-scale row out here in the midday heat? Me ranting at her, and her glaring back at me until we both collapsed with thirst and sunstroke? No, thanks.

I could have simply ignored her, of course. Like she was ignoring me. Gone and got my stuff out of the tent and told her I was leaving.

Or gone and got my stuff – and just wandered off without telling her.

Or just wandered off for a while.

Then, when I was back, I'd wait for a more suitable departure time.

And so, with a silent and rather pathetic shake of the head, I left her where she sat, biting her lips and digging her nails into her palms. She glared up at me from her chosen spot in the full-force sun. Probably she would stay there for hours and fry her brains, I thought to myself. OK, then let her.

After a drink of water and a cooling face-wash, I made my way back up the slope and set off along the track. I went in the opposite direction from before, this time towards Buena Suerte. I could go anywhere I wanted: I could join Toni for a swim; I could follow the river and see where it took me; I'd been told that a kind of hermit lived at the top of the hill on the far bank – I could always pass by and check him out. There were all kinds of possibilities. I'd consider it as taking a last look round this unspoiled paradise before heading back to real life in the twenty-first century.

Less than ten minutes later I was again sticky with sweat and dunned into almost a stupor by the heat. I should have worn a hat. I should have brought some water. The path I was on would soon bring me to Mad Marshall's. No matter. Once I came to the wood above his place I'd turn off into the shade. That was the plan.

After walking a little further, I stopped to watch a family of rabbits bound down the slope and cross the open ground towards the river. I carried on and a short time later came in sight of the Marshall property up ahead, precisely the place I wanted to avoid.

But there on my left was the wood – right on cue.

I was about to turn off the path when I heard someone shout. Not at me, though, thank God. The schoolboy pioneer was jumping up and down in the dirt yard in front of his cabin. Throwing a tantrum, by the looks of things, waving his arms like a windmill, stamping his feet and bellowing. Seated under the Martini umbrella as before, and paying no attention to him, was Rosa.

That brief glimpse of their domestic life was enough – I left the path, hoping to bypass the pair of them altogether. The deeper I went into the wood the fainter became Marshall's shouting until finally I could hear only birdcalls, the occasional *ruiseñor* making liquid sweet music nearby or the harsh call from a *gach*... and in the distance what might have been the rapid tap-tap-tap of a woodpecker. As I passed, one of the *gach* rose into the air, making a clatter of wings like a clumsy pigeon, then, as it flew past me, I saw that this dull brown bird, its wings spread out, was streaked with metallic blue and black. Quite unexpected beauty.

When I emerged I hadn't quite reached the far edge of the property, a slight miscalculation. In Anna-speak, of course, I had *meant* to emerge precisely where I did – according to her, no one ever 'miscalculated'. Oh, yes? Whatever, I had no reason to go down there and no wish to meet either of them – not mad-eyed Marshall, nor burned-out Rosa. Not, anyway, as far as I knew.

Yet down I went.

The midday sun had settled to a deadening weight on my head and shoulders. Having zigzagged through the dry crackle of long grass, I reached the boundary fence. There was no one in sight. An easy climb over the wire, a cautious approach of fifty metres or so across open ground – making a slight detour to go round a collapsed heap of rusted pipes tangled with weeds and butterflies, the heat pulsing out from the metal as I passed it – and I had reached the cabin door.

I came to a halt.

Was it my conscience that made me picture Thérèse as she would be at that moment: sitting exactly as I had left her, basting her sullenness in the heat? Probably, because I should have been with her, comforting her, trying to talk to her, trying to leave her, even – anything might have helped her at that point. Anything except walking off to go and creep round someone else's house like a thief.

No sign of Rosa. The hillside opposite was in haze. By squinting into the glare I could just make out Marshall, his back to me, scything some dead-looking long grass at the far edge of his property. I knocked on the door, but not too loudly.

I waited, listened. Then knocked again.

No reply.

Marshall's faint outline rippled back to me through the heat as his scythe swung and cut, swung and cut. Then, almost as if I was watching myself doing it, I turned the door handle and stepped inside.

Was this to be the high spot of my farewell sightseeing: the tour of a genuine native house and a sneak look at genuine native lifestyle – one last glimpse, before heading back to civilisation?

With the only window shut and its blind pulled down, the room was like an oven. Not a breath of clean air, yet there was an unexpected calm, a sense of refuge from the insect noise and the harsh sun.

The interior was a few notches up from the abandoned *finca*; the roof looked intact. There was a blind, but it was so threadbare that, where it had rotted through, slashes of light burned into the unpainted walls and ceiling; the old-fashioned bed with its massive headboard was a heap of grubby sheets and someone's washing – underwear, frayed towels and filthy sweatshirts. Elsewhere was a clutter of tangled rope, paint tins, boxes of nails and screws, boots, shoes and batteries. Several dozen tins – ham, baked beans and frankfurters mostly – were stacked on a carton marked CHILLI CON CARNE in one corner; a sledgehammer leaned in the other. The only neat thing in the room was what looked like a sketch-plan nailed to the wall. Lettering large enough to read from where I stood announced: PARADISE.

My shirt stuck to my back, sweat was trickling down my legs. I picked my way through the debris for a closer look.

It was the plan Toni had told me about: a genuine nibbed-pen, black-ink-and-ruler job – every line drawn with schoolboy exactness. The paper was yellowed from the harsh sunlight and the ink faded, but the rectangles of different sizes could still be made out. They were labelled: HOUSE, MAIN SHED, GENERATOR SHED, GARAGE, PARKING, STABLES, TACK ROOM, TOOL STORE, SEED STORE, COWSHED, PIGSTY, HENHOUSE, APIARY, WOODSHED, KENNELS. Dotted lines enclosed areas marked out as VEGETABLE GARDEN, HERB GARDEN, ORCHARD, FLOWER GARDEN, SWIMMING POOL, PATIO. A black line DRIVE running from GARAGE to MAIN GATE was stopped there by double red lines. The boundary fence was shown in brown. Outside the fence there was no river marked, no neighbours, no woods, no track and no valley. Everything was drawn to a scale indicated in the bottom right-hand corner.

A woman's voice: 'Paradise five more year.' After a pause she added: 'Five year? Fifty year? Never.'

Rosa was standing in the shadows, just behind the door. She must have been there all the time, watching me. She was completely naked.

'*Sí*, the Paradise plan.' She stepped forward into the light, and I saw that her body was bruise-marked at the shoulder. A purple weal. I tried to look away. She seemed older than before, her face burned to near darkness, faint wrinkles round her mouth and eyes. Her hair was loosely pinned up at one side.

'Paradise joke, *claro!*'

She turned slightly. I must have been staring at the bruise, for she said: 'You see me?'

Finally I managed to say something: 'Mmm, uh-huh.'

She brushed a stray fall of hair from the side of her face and pointed, almost shyly, over to the bed. 'You are here because you want that we…?'

I didn't believe I was hearing right – but then I hardly believed I was seeing right either. Her naked breasts, her thighs. So I looked away…

…And found myself picturing Anna. *She* wouldn't have just turned away. She'd have talked to Rosa. Asked her what had happened, how she had got the bruise, been sympathetic. Anna was nothing if not sympathetic. But it wouldn't have stopped there; she'd have wanted to touch the wound, to be reassured it wasn't her own – to be certain that the pain she could see being suffered wasn't hers.

Was it only a couple of months since I'd abandoned Anna at the Gare du Nord? A couple of lifetimes, more like.

On the shelf above their bed slumped a line of tattered dictionaries and catalogues. The colours of a polished stone were bleeding into the surrounding wood. Next to it, an old-fashioned wooden barometer nailed to the wall showed FAIR – I felt an almost irresistible urge to tap the glass.

'Marshall not here. He make Paradise. No worry.' She didn't smile. 'You want?' She sat on the edge of the bed and looked up at me. 'You not want?'

There was a scrabbling overhead as a bird landed on the metal roof. Rosa gave no sign of having heard it. I stood still, not knowing what to do or what to say. With a kick, the bird lifted itself free.

'Rosa, I— '

'We make love, I say. No talk. No name.'

To avoid staring at her, I glanced over at the map again. There was a matchstick couple standing outside the house; they were holding hands.

'*Hombre! Qué quiere?* You want? You not want?'

She had stood up again. There was a dry cracking sound in my throat as I swallowed. I didn't know what to say.

She shrugged, then pulled back a loose strand of hair.

She took a step nearer. I stepped back, stumbling over one of the boxes.

A moment later, all but blinded by the fierceness of the sun, I was scrambling up the slope. Some hundred or so metres away, Marshall continued methodically scything the grass – he hardly seemed to have moved.

7

Back on the red-dirt track, I paused to get my breath. If I'd had my passport and bank card with me, that would have been the moment to have headed straight for Buena Suerte.

Instead, it was back to Toni's shack. Back to Thérèse.

From the grim silence of her greeting, nothing had changed. OK, fine by me. What would be the point of trying to talk to her? I gave her a distant nod – which was ignored – then I strode past. I continued towards the tent.

I'd get things ready so I could leave the first chance I got.

'Jack?'

I kept on walking.

I was now a good dozen steps beyond her. A glance back

out of the corner of my eye: she looked miserable.

'Jack. Not walk away. Please.'

'Yes, Thérèse?'

'I know I really hurt you...'

I nodded.

This was more like it. No better balm for the bruised soul than some hardcore grovelling.

'Sometimes everything in me gets mixed up: my parents, my father. It is not you to blame. I am very sorry.'

I smiled to indicate the possibility of forgiveness. She began smiling in return, grateful and obedient. She held out both hands. 'Help me?'

So I did, and she got to her feet.

She explained how when she was falling asleep everything had seemed hopeless; when she woke up she decided to set off with Charlie in the Toyota. At first she'd been really sad and angry. No, she'd no idea where she was going – Paris, the Holiday Village Apartments and her parents? She couldn't think of anywhere. Then, a few kilometres down the road, she'd got out and walked all the way back. She was very, very sorry.

We kissed and made up. Easy as that. No need for the big talk. No need to leave, not immediately anyway.

The keynote of togetherness struck, we decided to have a spontaneous picnic. As well as the biscuits and fruit for an idyllic *déjeuner sur l'herbe* we took some sacking to keep the biters, wrigglers and crawlers out of our hair.

Soon we were sitting down by the bathing pool stretch of the river, the current's slow trickling *arpeggio* over the loose stones providing background Muzak for our feast.

Short term at least, everything would be perfect: the warm

breeze, the rippling water, the birdsong, our togetherness. Feeling bad about how close I'd come to abandoning her earlier, I wondered about making it into a joke: I could say that the two of us were so much in love that, even if we wanted to separate, we just couldn't do it.

I was about to begin telling her how near I myself had come to leaving – *What a day! You start by leaving me, and then I…* – when she spoke first.

'I lie to you.'

'Pardon?'

'When I say my father not know who I really was, I told you very big lie.'

'What?'

'I tell him what is true. I tell him I am his daughter.'

There was a pause that even the warm breeze, the rippling water and the birdsong round us couldn't fill.

'I told him, just before he… before he died.'

'What? In his very last moments?'

She nodded.

'How could you be so… so cruel?'

'No. You not understand. I wasn't cruel. No. It was not like that, Jack.' She paused. 'It was worse, very worse.'

'Worse? How the hell could it be worse?'

'You not understand, Jack. You not want to understand.'

Then she clammed up. She began trembling; her whole body had started shaking. I tried to hold her, to calm her.

She pushed me aside, screaming: 'Let me go! Leave me alone. LEAVE ME ALONE!'

Struggling free, she jumped to her feet and ran off down the banking and into the river. Midway across, she stood in the water, quite still, her arms held high, her hands clenched into fists. All at once, throwing back her head, she howled out loud enough to fill the valley. Then followed a long-drawn-out retching of breath that came slower and deeper until, finally, she fell to her knees. Still gasping for air, she bowed herself down and thrust her head under the surface.

Though all this was happening right in front of my eyes, it took me a couple of seconds to realise what she was trying to do. Then I rushed into the water, slipping on the loose stones and weeds. The river wasn't deep – I splashed my way to her, grabbed her under the arms and pulled. She came up gasping, choking; her hair and her face were streaming with water. I hauled her on to her feet, then dragged her kicking and spluttering back on to the bank.

Having laid her on the sacking, I sat down beside her, stroking her hair, the side of her face, her arms, the back of her hands, while she quietened down. She was sobbing to herself, almost silently.

My departure would have to be postponed.

8

Our life together had reached an all-time low. We hardly talked. I had tried and she had tried, but after that last attempt ended so badly Thérèse clammed up for good. Anna would have nagged and therapised her wide open, but I let her be. This act of cowardice I called *being tactful*. We lived out a kind of half-hearted truce. Most mornings she'd sleep late, then wander off by herself, usually coming back after a few hours and looking fractionally brighter. Most nights I held her until she fell asleep. I could just about manage that.

The days passed, the weeks passed – we hardly noticed. Charlie drove to Vic and returned with supplies. We'd swim in the river. I learned to ride a horse, sort of. Evie was plump and small, more of a low white wall than a pony, and as likely to move. Maybe she'd been one of the wild bunch in her youth, but with the daily oats of captivity she'd spread herself and it always took a fairly firm boot to get her moving. A series of fairly firm boots later, she'd amble forward a few metres, then stop for a snack. That was her compromise: so many metres, so many mouthfuls. It was easier walking. Sometimes, as we strolled along the track above Paradise, we saw Marshall toiling away with his breeze blocks and cement, and maybe Rosa helping him – more often she'd be sitting in the shade of the umbrella. We'd wave and might get a wave back; then again we might not. The weather had got slightly chillier in the mornings and slightly colder at nights. Better for sleeping, if nothing else. When the sun was full, it was as hot as ever. Some evenings, just for the fun of it, we built a fire down by the river, Charlie's guitar leading us in a communal singsong. Toni's 'big surprise', the abandoned *finca*, had not been mentioned again.

We were having breakfast one morning when we heard the rumble of an engine from along the track. Someone was coming to call. A rare event. I'd been wondering how to make this day a bit different from the previous ones, which had involved a lot of sitting around and not much else. I'd been inspired by a change in the weather: instead of the usual clear skies, there was a dampness in the air, and clouds were already building up.

More out of boredom than any passionate desire for hard work, I had just suggested that I borrow some tools from the pioneering gnome down the road – then Toni and I could do some repairs on their shack. We could surely fix things so that at least a few of the wrigglies and most of the rain would be kept out? Thérèse was sitting next to me. She was drinking tea and crumbling up a biscuit, every now and again licking the crumbs from her fingers. This was as much as I knew about what was going on in her life.

At the sound of vehicle, Toni got to his feet. 'I think Marshall comes.'

A dozen metres or so from where we were sitting I saw the mad-eyed pioneer's Toyota shudder to a halt in a cloud of red dust. My first thought: was Rosa with him? Over Thérèse's shoulder I watched Marshall climb out of the passenger seat, slam the door and begin to make his way towards us. Toni went to meet him.

At that distance, and with the rain clouds gathering, it was too dim to see into the cab. Marshall was talking and pointing back along the track. Surely Rosa wouldn't have said anything about my turning up at their shack that time? I could almost smell that closed room again, the stifling heat, the violence lingering in the grubby sheets like static.

Thérèse leaned towards me. Without lowering her voice, she said: '*C'est bien dit* what you say – he is like a gnome.'

Marshall glanced over in our direction but didn't seem to have heard. He simply gave us a nod of greeting. Next to Toni, he looked even shorter and stockier, his beard adding to the general gnominess.

I was reaching to take Thérèse's hand and give it a squeeze

in token of our sharing this opinion of our neighbour, and in acknowledgement of a rare sign of life on her part, when she turned away. Instead, I kissed the back of her neck. Maybe this was her coming out of her depression? If she was no longer depressed, then everything was all right. Maybe it had all been grief and, at last, she was recovering. Her father was dead – end of that story. Her parents were a write-off – end of story number two. Surely we could now start again? I would draw an invisible circle round us both and call what lay inside story number three.

The pick-up's other door slammed and Rosa appeared.

That she'd showed up at that very moment made me all but hate her. Already she was threatening to disturb the newly imagined invisible circle that was going to protect Thérèse and me and keep us safe. Nothing had really happened in that grimy cabin, of course, but I had no idea what Rosa might say, or do, or tell. I wanted to get Thérèse away from there as quickly as possible. I really believed in that invisible circle, and my responsibility was to get story number three up and running. Charlie had been talking earlier about the wild horses down at the river. As good an excuse as any. I got to my feet and, interrupting Thérèse in mid-chat with Charlie, took her hand in a playful tug.

'Let's not get caught up in the social whirl! A polite wave, and we'll go to see the horses.' I put my arm round her shoulder, intending to lead her away.

Rosa leant against the front of the Toyota. She was wearing a check shirt with the sleeves rolled half up, and baggy jeans. At first there was no sign she'd even noticed us; to all appearances, she was the patient wife waiting for her rather talkative husband. No suggestion of the woman I had previously seen naked and bruised. Standing with one foot resting on the bumper, she began rolling a cigarette.

Thérèse and Charlie carried on talking. I watched Rosa light up, then turn to face us.

A split second too late I looked away; she had caught my eye and was coming towards us. I gave Thérèse's shoulder a squeeze. 'We should move off, eh?'

At once she stiffened. 'I am talking with my friend Charlie.'

'Yes, but if we want to see the horses...'

'Why the big rush? We see them before.'

'Rosa!' Marshall had called out to his wife. She came to an abrupt halt only a few metres short of us.

'*Sí, señor?*' she answered in a mock-submissive voice, making everybody laugh. I joined in.

'You know we're in a hurry. Come on, back into the truck.'

Still playing the long-suffering wife, she raised her eyes to heaven: '*Sí, señor.*'

On her way back to the Toyota she walked past him and blew smoke into his face. Then she climbed in, switched on the engine; the pick-up rolled slowly forward.

'Shit!' Marshall broke off his goodbyes, rushed up the slope, then ran along the track beside the Toyota, trying to grab hold of the door handle. Finally he managed to clamber into the moving cab – and everyone laughed as they drove off leaving a thick dust cloud like red mist hanging in the air.

Thérèse picked up a large stick from the woodpile and hurled it after the disappearing truck.

'That's for crazy love!' she shouted.

Already the day was darkening, the air becoming heavier,

stickier. Our near-silent look at the horses was followed by a wordless walk back to the shack. In what seemed like no time at all we were sitting exactly the same as before. Thérèse's depression had returned. Whenever I went to take her hand she drew away.

Once again I brought up the subject of some DIY. We could secure the windows a bit better, I pointed out, like screw them into some frames; we could hang the door so that it opened and closed properly; fix a few leaks.

At the last suggestion Charlie seemed interested: 'Yes, it's probably going to rain soon.'

'Good. Let's go for it!' I said, trying to get everyone into the swing of things.

Thérèse glanced up: 'Why is it good to rain?'

'Then we can find out where the leaks are.'

'Toni knows now where are the leaks. Better you mend them before the rain.'

For a moment Mr FixIt felt like fixing her with a firm but therapeutic suggestion to shut the fuck up.

While Thérèse had been refusing to communicate, I'd written a postcard to my mother, so I was a good son. I was going to help mend my hosts' roof, so I was a good guest. I was not going to shout at Thérèse, so I was a good boyfriend. I had to be good, not having the courage to be anything else.

I got to my feet. 'We'll need tools. I'll go over to Marshall's.'

'He is away to collect wood,' said Toni.

'Maybe he'll be back by the time I get there.'

I had to move, I had to do something.

As I left, Thérèse called after me: 'Say my love to the gnome.'

9

I'd gone only a few steps when I decided that, all things considered, paying a second visit to the Marshall homestead probably wasn't such a great idea. I'd try the woman Dolores instead. Of course, I'd have to explain who I was. But she'd probably have tools.

This was the first time that I'd returned so far back along the track since arriving here in the valley. Had that been a month ago, two months? Even longer? I had no real idea. All I knew for certain was that a heavy rain was coming and I'd soon be getting soaked to the skin. Even the red dust on the road was sluggish underfoot; the grass and shrubs were glossed over by the light and seemed further away than they should be. The air tasted damp and vaguely metallic.

With a sense of being, for once, in the right place at the right time, and doing the right thing, I strode along the track in my search for tools to fix a leaking roof. At last, I was following in my father's footsteps: Mr McCall the roofer, Jack McCall the roofer's son! I laughed out loud. It was a moment's light-heartedness.

The right place? The right time? Doing the right thing? Like always as I walked along the track, each step seemed to be the next one, the only one to take. The sky was blue-grey going on black, the air breathless and almost dripping to the touch. The track was rising very slightly. Dolores's place lay about a kilometre ahead. This light-hearted walk was the calm before the storm.

*

She was working in one of the vegetable patches when I arrived. Beside where she was kneeling, a plastic bag lay flat on the ground, a few newly cut courgettes neatly stacked on it. A dozen or so hens were scrabbling nearby, pecking at the dirt. When I called out to her, they flapped and scrambled to take themselves a few metres further off. She looked up – a rather pretty woman in a small and untidy sort of way. Most of her was a swathe of light-coloured hair and a smile. We shook hands and did the me Jack, me Dolores bit. She spoke schoolgirl English.

'You like see Miguel?' she invited.

We went indoors. The cabin floor was like the surface of a sea on which floated a scatter of toys, books, papers, clothes and shoes. She kicked aside the flotsam to reach her small slip of a child who had been set sailing to sleep in a large drawer awash with rags.

'This – Miguel.'

A bundle of dark blue cotton topped off with two eyes, a nose and a grin. She lifted him up.

'Miguel walk soon!'

We returned outside to sit on the top step and keep an eye on the dark clouds piling themselves higher and higher across the valley. Some baby talk followed between Dolores and Miguel. Having asked the customary questions, I moved into children's entertainer mode. My repertoire is largely non-verbal: a popping sound made by putting my fingers in my mouth; then, for the more mature child, 'Here's the church, and here's the steeple/Open the doors, and here's the people' with my hands. Best of all is a farting noise I make by forcing a vacuum between my cupped palms – this goes down well with all ages. Miguel was my first failure; he began screaming aloud in alarm. Dolores asked me to hold him while she tried it herself.

Afterwards, Miguel was put into a hammock of sacking and twine, swinging an occasional gurgle from between the rusted yellow van and a fig tree. Turning down the offer of coffee and dope, I moved on to business. We discussed tools: it seemed she herself borrowed them as required from Marshall, who was only a fifteen-minute short cut down the slope opposite. Or, more exactly, Sven borrowed them; it was too far for him to carry his own tools from his place up on the hill. From time to time he would come and fix things for her: the generator which had packed up a month or so back, or getting rid of a wasps' nest, replacing a broken window and the like.

'For thank you, I fix something for him – and always same thing!' she laughed.

Another few finger-pops with Miguel, and it was time to go.

Having closed the gate, I turned to give her a final wave, but she was already seeing to Miguel. The sky was black; the air had turned electric.

The storm was about to start.

Long before I could get back to Toni's shack the rain would be hammering down. Then what? I'd be soaked to the skin and, thanks to my not having brought back any tools, the four of us would be sitting in that one room, not moving to keep clear of the drips. There'd be buckets, pots and basins pinging away on all sides; the dampness would bring out clouds of mosquitoes and other biters. There'd be bits of sodden sacking and torn plastic crammed into gaps round the window frames and doors. Or else, knowing DIY Toni, he'd just let the rain pour in. Also, there'd be no avoiding Thérèse and her sullen silence. Whatever, it was either the four of us in a one-room sieve or me and Thérèse sardined together in the wet tent.

Forget it.

Better to be completely on my own. In the abandoned *finca* perhaps: the clapped-out ex-pianist and the clapped-out piano keeping each other company. The back room had looked reasonably watertight. I'd take the long way round, skirting past Marshall's, keeping close to the river bank as I passed near Toni's place. If I kept out of sight, and went a bit further than usual, I could edge myself up the slope and on to the track leading to the farmhouse – coming at it from the far side so as not to be seen by anyone.

Downpour over, I'd return to the sieve and make a real effort to get story number three started.

No problem.

I hurried off down the slope leading to the river. Already, the air seemed to be running with damp, making Marshall's cabin look like a wet cardboard box left out in the rain. No Toyota in the space marked PARKING and nobody in sight. Maybe the two of them were rushing back home at that moment to have a cosy afternoon together: him with his shorts, beard and fists, her with her bruises?

I cut along the back fence of their property, stepped down into the gully and started to walk along by the river.

I was not alone for long. I had reached the small wood beyond where Toni's shack stood on the slope above.

'*Hola!*' A few metres to my right, leaning against a fallen tree trunk, was Rosa. She nearly smiled.

I didn't smile back.

The air was thickening by the minute and the surface of the water had curdled to a leaden dullness. Blue-black clouds were stacked up above the hill, while the rest of the sky seemed a hazy colourlessness crisscrossed by birds darting this way and that. She came towards me. 'Where your girlfriend?'

I mumbled something about Thérèse feeling very tired, probably because of the approaching storm, and that she had wanted to lie down.

'You think? Come.' She strode off, clearly expecting me to follow.

I stayed where I was. Small animals scrabbled round me in the undergrowth. A half-dozen or so of the wild horses had gathered on the opposite bank, whinnying and tossing their heads, watching us. There was no real sunlight any more, just an after-brightness so strained by the massing clouds as to have no particular source and no shadow. Everything looked unnaturally sharp-edged and flat. The first heavy drops fell.

'No make love, no worry.' Rosa had returned to my side. She took my arm, jerking me a few steps forward. 'Come. No *lejos*. Not far. Come.'

Just then, with a sudden clattering, tearing sound on the leaves, the storm broke. Almost instantly the rain deluged down. A real torrent, like a tropical cloudburst. We were soaked through in seconds. Rosa had to shout to make herself heard. 'You must come. You must come.' She grabbed my shirt and pulled hard. I had to follow; it was either that or starting a fight over it.

The two of us squelched and skidded along the mud path

that slithered between the trees. I shielded my eyes against the downpour, but she didn't bother. Her hair hung in a wet mass with black rat-tail strands stuck across her face.

'Like the day Marshall and me first here,' she shouted above the rain. 'Fucking monsoon, and he goes walk-walk-walk in rain with his stones. Put here one stone, there one stone. For *rincón*, he say, to mark corner of our house, of stables, of every building. Four stones for workshed, four stones for garage, four stones for swimming pool. I hear very often these fucking words. House, stables, workshed, garage, swimming pool.' She paused, then continued: 'That first day there is only rain everywhere, only mud everywhere. Stones everywhere. Stones for Paradise fuck-up.'

She halted abruptly and tugged the hair back from her face. 'I stay in the van, such loud rain on roof. Such noise. I watch. Stone. Mud. Patio. Swimming pool. I think him brave. I think him good man.' She stared straight at me: 'But he is not really good now – now he is *loco rematado*. Complete crazy.'

She nearly slipped and clung to my arm to keep her balance. By then we were clambering up the slope, like wading through a waterfall. To the right was a derelict wooden shack, rotted and with most of the roof missing; a tattered strip of plastic flapped where the window should have been. There was no front door.

'Soon everyone who come here go very crazy.' She pointed towards the shack but kept walking. 'That man is shot.'

'What?'

'He shoot himself in head,' she yelled into my ear. 'Many come here like that. Crazy when they come – then worse. Nothing here for them, not like in the big city. Only them and their craziness.' She pointed high in the air on the opposite bank. 'Sven, the man who live alone up on the hill, he not violent crazy but calm crazy. *Entiende?*'

I didn't understand but nodded anyway.

She shouted back: 'But that is not what I show you. It is something else to see. Something not good. Nearly there. We must go quick.'

We had come out of the wood and were looking across to the empty *finca*, or what we could see of it through the driving rain. The air was still sticky and warm. Grabbing at the clumps of long grass, we pulled ourselves up the short slope where the path had become little more than a mudslide. We would have to slog a further three hundred metres to get to the farmhouse, if that's where we were going.

10

Though the rain was thundering off the metal sheeting that patched a section of the roof, Rosa signalled for me not to make a sound. She tiptoed up the front steps and waved for me to follow. Someone had removed the string that held the front door shut, but instead of pushing it open to get herself in out of the rain she took my arm and started to draw me round the side of the building. The wooden veranda was slippery, so we had to tread cautiously. At every step, dirty rainwater oozed up between the planks.

Round the back was Marshall's Toyota, stacked with wood that was getting drenched.

We stopped and for a moment stood side by side looking across the valley. As she put her arm round me, her warmth seeped into my body. She didn't seem to notice the rain streaming down her face. She raised her hand and drew it down the side of my cheek, but there was no affection in the gesture, no tenderness. She pulled me towards the window.

Suddenly I wanted nothing of this.

Who cared what went on between her and Marshall? Him, a mad bastard? She was pretty freaky herself. Maybe they'd set this up between them: her going out to capture me, like some innocent, and bringing me here for whatever weird pleasures they were into. She was standing behind me now, her arms hugging my chest so that I couldn't free myself without a struggle.

'You must look,' she hissed into my ear loud enough to be heard above the frantic pounding of the rain.

The shutter was rusted firmly in place. I did my best to peer between the slats. At first, because of the grubby window and the poor light, I could make out only smudges on the glass against the dimness behind. Rosa was pressing herself hard against me now, her breasts pushing into my back and her hands holding on to me, her fingers digging into my chest. The rain was trickling off her hair on to the side of my face.

'Now you can see?'

An abrupt movement in the room caught me by surprise, and I saw Marshall kneeling on the floor. Then I saw the old mattress, a looming mass in the dinginess; it was covered by the green tarpaulin sheet from his pick-up, tarpaulin that should have been keeping his wood dry. There was a quick blur as someone walked by only centimetres away, just inside the window, and went over to him.

'Easy. I hold you.' I heard Rosa's voice as if it was coming from a hundred miles away.

I had recognised the rainbow hair first, falling across the older man's face. The gnome, she'd called him. *Say my love to the gnome,* she'd said.

We must have returned along the veranda, gone down the steps and back along the path – but it was not until we were again in the wood and sitting under a tree that I could really start to take in what I had just seen. I felt very shaky, very much alone. Rosa was next to me; she'd taken a tin box out of her pocket and was rolling a small joint. I watched her lick the paper, tight-twist the end and light it. She looked at me. 'You OK?'

Then I saw the scene in that house again: Marshall and Thérèse embracing, naked.

'Here.' She passed the joint over.

I didn't talk and neither did she. After a few minutes she rolled another.

Later, when the rain had stopped, we watched Thérèse leave the house, walk along the path and disappear where it curved to join the main track back to Toni's. It seemed to take her an unending length of time.

Still feeling stoned I kept missing my footing on the path, while above me the stars slid in and out of position. From the darkness on either side came the sounds of night creatures, stifled and abrupt.

I should have been planning what to say to Thérèse, but it took all my concentration to lift and place one foot in front of the other. Every so often I'd stand perfectly still as though waiting for something. After several deep breaths, the stars would look a little steadier and the ground feel less shifting. Then I'd carry on. But all I could see in front of me was Thérèse's hand resting on Marshall's bare shoulder and the fanning open of her hair as she leaned down to kiss him.

Finally I caught sight of the candle burning in the shack window. I'd been gone for nearly half the day. Would Thérèse sit and say nothing, continuing her pretence of a bad mood, or would she be all smiles and friendliness? Which would be worse?

Who cared? I had just been given the perfect reason for leaving.

Toni looked up from where he'd been crouched blowing into the cooking fire. 'Storm not good for walking, eh?'

I told him about seeing Dolores for the tools and being sent to Marshall's. There was no one there, so I'd wandered off into the wood to take shelter from the rain – and got a bit lost. It was the truth, near enough.

'Sorry about the tools,' I added.

Thérèse was sitting in one of the old car seats. 'Easier to find shack in the dark?'

I didn't say anything. Deception's a disease like any other, and easily caught.

After dinner it began to rain again. Another real downpour. If the weather cleared up next day, I'd be off. For a short while we sat huddled beneath the tarpaulin, but soon there was water coming in everywhere and we retreated inside the shack. It was drier, marginally. Thérèse sat on one end of the bed and read a tattered French paperback. Charlie sat on the other and played the guitar. Toni and I sat on the floor and played chess. There was no conversation as the rain thundered on to the corrugated-iron roof. All evening we listened to it dripping and splashing and pinging into the pots and pans. Cockroaches scuttled about in the dim corners, small scorpions sidled past us and winged and multi-legged things hopped, fluttered and flopped their way across our candlelit board.

11

By midnight the storm had blown itself out and the rain had stopped. Everything was calm and still. Thérèse and I made our way in silence to the tent. Without speaking, I crawled into my sleeping-bag. Thérèse had already climbed into hers and lay with her back to me.

'Goodnight, *dors bien*,' she said in a sleepy-sounding voice.

'Goodnight.'

When she shifted her weight slightly, the foot of her sleeping-bag brushed against mine. I drew back.

There was the hollow, rumbling sound of some wild horses cantering along the river bank. The thud of their hooves made the ground tremble. All I could think was: Thérèse had been naked and giving herself to that gnome all afternoon. I wanted to shout, to scream at her.

I began: 'You were with Marshall this afternoon.'

Staring into the darkness, I waited for her response.

And waited, and waited.

Finally I sat up on one elbow: 'Well?'

'Well – what?'

'You and Marshall.'

She was keeping her back to me. I put my hand on her shoulder and wrenched her round to face me.

'You and Marshall!' I could just about see her face in the darkness.

'It happen.'

The casualness of her reply was all I needed.

'You just happened to find yourself in bed with him?' As I leaned nearer, I could sense her withdrawing. 'You just happened to leave here without telling anyone, went into that old house where he just happened to have gone as well. What with the rain and no TV and the piano needing tuning, you just happened to fuck instead?'

I could feel her breath on my cheek. I felt strong and, most of all, I felt in the right. There's no high like the high of justified anger. 'Was today the first time?'

'It is not important.'

'And you and me? Did that just happen too?'

No reply.

'In Paris. You remember Paris? When you and I ended up in your bed, did that just— '

She sat up and faced me, suddenly angry: 'Yes, Jack, I remember Paris. I remember how you want a place to stay. And how you want someone, anyone. That is all. So, yes, Jack, it happen.'

Our faces were very close, almost touching. I hissed at her: 'That was all? You bitch! You fucking bitch!'

A moment later I was on top of her, pressing my whole weight down. To crush her. I wanted to hear her cry out in pain. Her hair was lying spread under my hand; I tugged it.

'Bitch! You fucking bitch!'

She caught her breath.

I tugged again.

She cried out. I clamped my hand over her mouth.

That's when I realised I was getting hard and, for the first time in weeks, felt charged and really alive. She was biting my fingers. I tugged again and tried to pull my hand free, but she grabbed my arm and kept biting. I kicked myself out of my sleeping-bag and unzipped hers. Within seconds we were biting and scratching at each other.

I had just entered her when, between half-sobs, she managed a breathless whisper: 'Yes, Jack... Yes... Take me, take me... TAKE ME!'

Immediately we awoke next morning, we began again. Wrestling and tugging, clawing and biting, fucking even more violently.

Afterwards we lay drenched in the sea-green light coming through the tent walls. A moment's tenderness.

Not quite the start to story number three that I'd imagined.

12

During the following weeks we fucked two or three times a day, getting more violent each time. We'd be walking through the woods one minute, and the next be playing at chase, running between the trees, splashing in and out of the river, trying to grab each other – all the while yelling at the tops of our voices. Moments later we'd be wrestling, rolling over and over in the mud and dust. We'd be slapping, pulling hair, swearing, spitting, scratching and biting until one of us drew blood, until one of us submitted. Between fucks I wondered if she'd stopped seeing the gnome – wondered, but never asked. Fucking her seemed easier.

And so the time passed, the weather a little chillier some mornings, but only just. I sent my mum a Christmas card – *Feliz Navidad*. Charlie marked the days to be sure she would return to school on the right day. That aside, we lived.

One morning, while I was finishing breakfast, Thérèse and Charlie – her red hair streaming behind her like she'd set the hillside on fire – headed to the river with a water-bucket each. They rushed down the slope, laughing and shouting as they played tag, zigzagging towards the water. Evie lifted up her head to watch them go helter-skeltering past, then returned to her day-long meal. Thérèse's voice was the louder; she was screaming in her excitement. They started stripping off as they ran. Thérèse pulled off her T-shirt and hopped along on one leg to free herself from her shorts.

Soon the two sun-browned dots were trying their best to splash each other in the shallow trickle which was all that remained of the bathing pool – the back-to-normal depth after the storm having vanished weeks go, almost as quickly as it had come. I was still watching them when Toni strolled up to me. He was carrying an axe.

'You are the hero?'

I put down my mug. A hero – for going to chop some firewood?

'No problem.' I laughed. 'See me, see Braveheart! Scottish

heroes!'

'Axe or spade?' Toni smiled. 'The axe is for the hero.'

The axe it was, then. But what was the spade for? Digging out the roots, maybe? Toni paused, then pointed across the yard: 'She's giving birth soon.'

It took me a moment to get what he was talking about.

'You don't mean chopping wood at all. It's that snake.' Red-brown with a whitish belly, black stripes, scales and fangs. A two-metre length of silence, speed and muscle that I'd seen a couple of times. The whip snake that was supposed to be harmless.

He went on to explain that the woodpile was not the right place for her any more. He and Charlie had been keeping the shack door wedged shut for days, but the poor creature was always watching for her chance. He pointed towards the loose-fitting window. 'Last night she try to come in there. Our bed is very near.'

I was getting the idea, slowly. 'The axe – it's for the snake? For killing the snake?'

'I tell you, *amigo*, she not want to go away. She want to have place here for her eggs. Many eggs – and soon many snakes. For her young snakes she will fight.' He paused, adding: '*Claro*, I not want to kill her. But I not want our house with many snakes.'

I tried to sound casual. 'It will be dangerous?'

'Not usual dangerous, but this time is not usual.' Then Toni smiled that easy smile of his which was probably supposed to make me feel relaxed. '*Sí, esá peligroso*. But we must.'

He handed me the axe, then in gestures explained our plan of action: he would ram the spade on to her back to hold her

151

down while I swung the axe and cut off the head. *No problemo.*

We were still in the shade, but the sweat was running off me already.

We approached the snake's lair, the woodpile. Very, very slowly. We had to get it into the open. I could see it staring out at me, its eyes glittering and cold, deep in the half-dark of the stacked branches. Hero and Spademan each picked up a stick.

Toni poked on the right-hand side of the pile, I poked on the left. The snake retreated – or was it coiling itself up to spring? Did snakes spring?

More poking, more retreating. My poking was becoming more daring; I was thrusting the stick as far into the pile as I could. The stacked wood shifted slightly as we worked our way towards the centre. I clambered on to the wood itself and started pushing down.

'Come on out!' I shouted whenever part of its length went slithering further out of reach. 'Come on!'

Then all at once it was right in front of me, rearing up. I leaped from the pile and hit the ground, landing badly.

It was there to meet me. Fangs, red muscle and striped belly arching over me, hissing. I rolled to one side. Toni slammed the edge of the spade into its back. Pinned down, it strained to get at me. Toni shouted: 'Axe! Axe!'

I got to my feet and started swinging at empty air.

A chest-high arc of spitting, hissing fury, it kept lunging at me. Again and again.

Toni pressed all his weight down on to his spade.

'Axe! Axe! AXE!'

The snake twisted and slid, rippling itself a little freer every second.

Another swing. This time I connected.

'Hard, hard!'

A dart of tongue jabbed the air a few centimetres from my hand. I managed another glancing blow. Fangs like curved claws just missed me.

Another slash at it, then another. One edge cutting into its right eye. A sudden upward lunge and Toni pressed down with everything he'd got, but it was slithering free. More than fury now, it was completely maddened and its blood was streaming over the shiny scales. Another wild chop, and then another. The axe getting slippery in my hand.

Blinded by sweat, I began slashing madly, staggering round and round.

Then Toni's voice: 'OK. OK. *Terminado*. Finished! You stop now!'

For several seconds I stared at the blood-stickiness and yellow-green slime on my trainers, on my hands, the axe blade, the handle. Ice-cold sweat was running down my face and chest. I had started shaking from head to toe.

I went and sat down. Toni gave me some water. My every nerve was tingling and shorting, every tremble of my arm sent more water spilling out of the cup.

When the women came back, we told them the whole story, acting it out all over again. They were impressed, and so was I.

'Where is the snake now?' asked Charlie.

Good question. I looked at Toni, and he told us.

It seemed that once I'd cut it in two, the separate parts had continued sliding jerkily, blindly, from side to side. Then, when they'd finally stopped moving, we'd taken a lifeless section each, whirled them over our heads and let go, sending them lassooing high into the air to land far off in the undergrowth. Primal stuff. Didn't I remember?

Yes – all at once I did. And I could still see the piece I'd thrown: it hung there above me, arcing over the valley like a dark crack in the sky.

13

That night, after our hosts had gone to bed, I went for a stretch-out on the slope of ground just below our tent. As I lay pleasantly and post-heroically stoned, listening to the seamless racket of insects and staring up at the stars, I was aware of Thérèse coming to sit next to me.

At her approach the insects fell silent. She made no move to touch me. I kept gazing at the night sky to give her – in Anna-speak – *plenty of space*. Finally I heard her say, in a very hesitant voice: 'I kill him.'

I made no reply. Had I heard right? Kill? Kill who?

'Like I say, Jack… Before he died, *mon père*… I told him… told him I was his daughter.' She was looking straight in front of her, not at me, and struggling to speak. She'd manage a few words, and then pause as if gathering strength for a few more. I reached to take her hand. She didn't seem to notice.

'It was our first time together when we are not in Paris. We never sleep together until… until that night… It was the first time. We did – but not complete, *tu comprends*?… Not everything… I pretend… the innocent… the shy girl. I say I am too young… I say: Not on the first night.'

She turned to look at me but turned away again almost

immediately.

'When we arrive he gives me the necklace... Then I try... I try very hard... to say who I really am... I keep trying to say... Then we kiss... We kiss, that is all.'

I squeezed her hand. She responded slightly before continuing: 'In the morning – maybe we are more relaxed, maybe more like friends... We go out on the balcony... and... and...'

I put my arm round her. When I began to stroke her hair, she abruptly pulled back.

'No, Jack. I will speak now and say everything. Let me say everything.' She squeezed my hand. 'The balcony... We go out on the balcony... He shows me a barbecue that he made last year.' Then she started to cry. 'There was much snow on the metal and the bricks... and he says in summer it is perfect for us... When we come back...'

This time she let me pull her towards me. I stroked her hair. Soothingly I repeated her name over and over.

She swallowed. 'Then... then... I point to the mountains and ask him what they are called. He tells me every name. And then I tell him... I tell him...'

I could feel her whole body straining, as if she herself was struggling to emerge from that scene for the first time. She tried to take her hand away, but I kept a tight hold.

'I understand,' I said.

'No. You cannot.'

'Really, Thérèse,' I interrupted. 'I understand.'

She looked me in the face and repeated firmly: 'No. You cannot.' She turned away again and continued: 'Then I tell him. I say he is my father and I am his daughter. At first he thinks I am meaning it like a joke; that I am the young girl and he is the older man... Like a joke... But it is no joke, I tell him.

It is no joke…'

'No,' I agreed, but she didn't seem to hear.

'Then, *tout à coup*, he understands what I am saying. Now he believes. He is very, very shocked, and he turns to look round at me. Much too suddenly he turns to look at me – and he falls back. It was the shock… the terrible shock. He turns much too quickly, and he slips on the ice… *crash* into the glass door. He falls. His head hits hard on patio stone.' She paused for several seconds. 'I kill him. I kill *mon père… mon père…*'

We sat there in the darkness for quite a while longer. I kept stroking her hair and kissing the top of her head. We were together, weren't we? I whispered. Now she had told me everything, things would be all right. Every few minutes I looked up at the stars. They never moved.

14

From then on I cared for Thérèse as for an invalid – trying to protect us both from her pain and her distress. The rough sex helped – its violence passed for intimacy and affection between us. At last I could enjoy what felt like a valid role in life: I was needed, therefore I *was*. The fact that Thérèse was unlikely ever to be truly healed merely made me feel more secure. We fucked and fought together harder than ever and played out our roles of sinner and forgiver, sufferer and comforter, to the satisfying full.

One morning Toni suggested that I go with him for a long ride on the horses. 'Not on road or track,' he explained. 'Two-, three-hour ride through wild country. You will never forget.'

How right he was. It started well enough. As I had been riding Evie regularly every few days over the previous couple of months, she now did what she was told, more or less. We saddled up, mounted and set off.

The river was so low we didn't even need to find the fording point to cross.

Sitting hands-free in his saddle, Toni rolled a joint as we jogged up on to the opposite bank. A flock of multi-coloured chattering birds swooped down to check us out and then flew off. We passed the joint back and forth between us. Toni pointed up the track ahead of us.

'Sven – the man on top of the hill. His house is in middle of trees.'

'He is the hermit? The man who lives all alone?'

'Very alone. With a woman at first. Not now.'

He passed over the joint. We made our way up the hill, picking a path through the wood. The sun was at its highest when we reached the small timber shack standing at the very summit. It was a one-roomed box constructed from sawn-up tree trunks and branches stuck together with what looked like tar. The door was closed. There was a faint wind brushing through the leaves of the nearby trees. That was the only sound, a dry rustling that got no louder and no softer. Too high, or the wrong sort of trees? Whatever, there was no birdsong. Just that unending rustle, rustle, rustle. Relentless, like breath without life.

We dismounted.

'Sven make his house here to be near God.'

'Oh.'

'We will not make a visit. Sven not like visits from people. But to take some water is OK.'

A tin mug hung next to a plastic container set in the shade. We each drank a couple of mugfuls.

'How long has he lived here?'

'Too long.'

'But you and Charlie have been here a long time.'

'*Sí*, many years. But we live one day at a time.' Taking hold of Tombo's reins, he swung himself up into the saddle. 'We are here only one day!'

We rode down the far side of the hill. After a mile or so through open country we entered a small wood where, in almost complete silence, our horses picked their way over the unmarked green of the mossy floor – all we could hear was the leather-creak of our saddles and the occasional distant birdcall. After the trees' shade it was a shock to emerge a few minutes later into harsh sunlight again. A short ride took us to the river's edge; here the clattering of Evie and Tombo's hooves on the loose pebbles was returned to us as echoes from across the valley. It seemed to fix our position.

There was a moment of instant and delicious coolness when our horses stepped into the river and began wading across. For once, the river was not shallow – unfortunately it was too far from our shack to be a convenient swimming hole. Laboriously, Evie pushed through the slow-moving current, her unsteady steps making me sway from side to side. The afternoon scene that had lain reflected on its calm surface was soon trampled into a swirl of elemental browns, reds, greens and blues. About halfway across we stopped to let the horses drink. I stared down at the churned-up water that was already returning to its former stillness of green leaves, branches and sky. With our reflections rippling across the surface, there came an unexpected sense of belonging, of being part of everything I could see round me...

Drinking session over, Evie's first step shattered the scene once more – and we moved forward.

'Last year when we cross here, Tombo swim. But not this year, and not any more. Every day the water is always getting lower and lower. When there is no water, then we must leave.'

The horses staggered a little on the uneven river bed; as we stepped back on dry land, things became smoother again. We soon slipped into an easy jog-jog, moving into a slowish trot through more woodland where the trees were far enough apart for the sun to come slanting between. There was a cooling breeze on our damp clothes. I urged Evie to lumber forwards into a medium trot. Was this her at full speed? I kicked her flanks and shouted. Reluctantly she moved up a gear. Soon we reached the foot of a rocky hill. As the horses climbed, every step they took dislodged loose shale and sent it rattling down the slope. The noonday sun dried our wet jeans. The sky was cloudless and the air like silk. Once over the hill, we swung to the right and, breaking into a canter, Tombo went thundering off ahead, hooves flying, across a stretch of open country. I held on tight as Evie moved into third.

Luckily she soon had to slow down again when we came to an outcrop of trees and low branches. We picked our way through and eventually reached a clearing. Nearly two hours after we had first set off, Toni reined in and stopped. I reined in and kept going.

'Whoa, Evie! Whoa!' I shouted. She did, eventually.

We tethered the horses in the shade of a fig tree and sat down under another nearby. Time to have a rest, share a few figs and a stirrup joint before our ride home.

Several purple-ripe figs later, I closed my eyes and let the all-round sound effect of insects and birds seep into me; layer upon layer of sun heat seemed to spread and re-spread. Again I felt that luxurious sense of belonging. I could hear Evie and Tombo at their all-day breakfast and the *jangle-clink* of their bridle bits as they moved from one patch of scrub grass to the next.

The day had reached a point of perfection, and stopped.

And the two of us seemed to have stopped with it. Not stopped living but, as it were, stopped dying. Just for the briefest moment, or for ever…

We'd be going back a different way, a shorter one, Toni told me as we jogged side by side out of the clearing. He knew of a possible pool nearby where we could have a leisurely midday swim before returning, then we'd have done a complete round trip of the property. That, at least, was the plan.

Five minutes later we were making our way between the trees of another small wood, bending down every few metres to avoid low-hanging branches. Eventually we came out into the full sun once more to rejoin the red-dust trail, and a hundred metres later we passed between the two trees marking, I recognised, the boundary of the property. Beyond them we could see where the track dipped down into a stretch of stones, pebbles, weeds and trickling water. The ford could be clearly made out now just under the surface. The twin wheeltracks hardly seemed to vanish under water at all, before reappearing again between the two oil drums I'd noticed on that first day. We jog-trotted to the water's edge.

The river, a wash of deep blue, was marked only by the image of a white bird's passage high above, its glide recorded in perfect detail on the surface like one of Montmartre's would-be Impressionist paintings, only much better. This was pure light painted on to utter transparency, the reflected sky.

All at once, a dozen metres or so to our left, there was a sudden upward rush of water – and, as if completing the composition, a naked man rose miraculously out of nowhere, almost choking as he gasped for air. He must have gone under only seconds before we arrived.

He nodded over to us. He was starvation-thin.

Toni called back: '*Hola*, Sven. We will swim with you. This is Jack. He has come all the way from…'

At last, I was getting to meet the hermit, the mysterious Sven. I was about to greet him when he held his hand up for silence. His thin arms stretched out as though they were antennae; he had begun sniffing the air.

'You can smell it?'

Toni breathed deeply: '*Sí*. It is not strong, but yes.'

All I could smell was… air.

Sven was already struggling, still wet, into his clothes. 'We had better hurry. It is possible someone is in danger.' A Swedish accent and, as Toni had mentioned, very good English – but clearly this was no time for conversation.

Toni had reined Tombo round and called out: '*Arriba! Arriba!*' He cantered off.

I followed, taking more deep breaths. More air.

In less than a minute Sven had overtaken me, running in long, loping strides.

15

Ahead, clouds of thick, dark smoke were rising from beyond the edge of the wood. There was a stench of burning that even I couldn't miss. I forced Evie into a faster trot, awkwardly lurching from side to side while holding on to the saddle with both hands. I reached open ground in time to see clouds of black smoke belching out through the shuttered windows of the old *finca*. Then the smoke became flames. There was a roaring that got louder and louder as the fire took hold of the shutters themselves, then the roof beams at the eaves, and then the door. The air was acrid with burning.

Evie stumble-stepped down the slope while I leaned back in the saddle to keep from sliding off. The nearer I approached, the more I could feel the heat and hear the timbers cracking. From inside the building came a series of crashes as the doorways fell in, the rafters loosened and smashed to the ground. The flames were now coming through what was left of the roof. Leaving Evie tied up to a fence-post alongside Tombo, I walked the last thirty metres, trying to get as close as I could. Marshall's pick-up – the driver's door still hanging open – stood on the overgrown track where it must have braked to a sudden swerving halt. I found Sven and Toni standing next to Rosa. She was lying on the ground coughing and retching; her face was blackened with soot and dirt, her clothes torn.

They were asking her if there was anyone still inside.

She didn't seem to understand the question. She kept shaking her head, then she pointed to the burning house.

Her gesture had the power of magic: there was a sudden

crash as the main doorframe gave way and the door fell in, covering the flames. We all took several paces back. For a few seconds the fire seemed to pause, then it flared up stronger than ever. The wind changed direction, and we had to move further away.

Between us, Toni and I half-dragged, half-carried Rosa and laid her on the slope near the Toyota. Her hands tightly gripping ours, we watched the destruction of what had been the oldest house in the valley. From the direction of our shack, Charlie appeared.

Just then the centre beam collapsed, and the remains of the roof went seconds later; a wall of heat struck us as twenty-foot high flames roared out. When I shouted over the noise to ask Charlie where Thérèse was, she pointed in the direction of the pool.

'Swimming,' she shouted back. 'She's swimming.'

'Swimming? But surely she'd have noticed the...?' I turned to Rosa. 'Where's Marshall?'

No response. She didn't even glance up.

Despite the intense heat, a chill clamminess washed over me.

When I asked her for the second time, her fingers clenched mine even tighter. She looked at me but said nothing.

Toni rushed back to the shack to call for help on his mobile, and Charlie drove off to the beginning of the valley to help guide them. Just as she left, Dolores came along the track with Miguel in her arms. In time, the fire burned itself out enough for us to pick our way through the wreckage. Only the smoke-blackened walls remained, some standing, some partly collapsed; the rest of the place was a gutted ruin, completely roofless. Here and there spars of wood still smouldered.

Stamping our feet at every step to check that the half-burned joists would be strong enough to take our weight, Toni, Sven and I stepped into the thinning smoke, into the acrid smell and stickiness of burned matting, the flakes of ash rising and falling. Above was the open sky, round us the trees and scrub seen through a veil of drifting ash. The piano lay toppled on its back, the metal frame and the hammer rods twisted by the heat; the still-smouldering centre roof beam straddled it, pointing partly upwards like an abandoned seesaw. The sheets of corrugated iron from the roof were still too hot to touch, and the bucketfuls of river water we emptied on them threw up clouds of steam, gradually cooling them. It was when we were lifting one of them out of the way that we found Marshall's body.

I had to walk off to be sick. When I returned I was still shaking.

Only by the crescent-moon necklace she'd been wearing was I able to recognise Thérèse. Her skin had been scorched to blackness, and the bones were showing through. She lay in the middle of what had been the small back bedroom. Her arms stretched out as if to ward off the horror that must have been already overwhelming her. The searing heat, the choking smoke. The flames catching at her clothes, her hair, her skin.

From the moment Rosa began speaking, I didn't believe a word she said. She told us she'd been setting off for Buena Suerte because the pump had seized solid yet again. Marshall was supposed to be away laying down traps and she'd got fed up waiting for him to come back. She'd noticed the smoke just as she reached the main trail. She'd turned back at once and arrived to find the fire already raging at the back of the house. She couldn't get close enough to see into the window. She'd shouted, but there was no reply. She'd tried throwing on what water there was in the water-barrel, but it was no use. She forced her way into the front where the fire was starting to gain hold. The door of the back room seemed jammed. She tried pushing it, then battering at it using one of the broken planks from the veranda – but she was soon driven back by the heat. The fire was spreading. Suddenly the smoke was so bad she could hardly breathe, and she had to get outside again.

The fire had probably started, she explained, because Marshall was a heavy smoker and would often leave his cigarettes not properly stubbed out.

She told us all this, sitting with her back against the Toyota: she spoke in a monotone and kept staring straight ahead, her hands locked together, her fingers tangled in her lap. There were tears running down her face.

It was still light when Charlie returned with the police and an ambulance. Rosa managed to get to her feet when they approached. She told them the same story, almost word for word. I believed it even less the second time. Having stood beside Rosa during that rainstorm, watching Thérèse and Marshall fucking each other, there was no doubt in my mind what had really happened. Rosa must have crept up to the door, fixed it shut and set the place on fire. Then left them to burn.

But I said nothing. I stood and listened – and said nothing.

*

Time and again that night I built their room around me out of flames, anger and desire. The smell of smoke clung to my skin and hair. All that night I tasted it in my mouth. And only a hand's breadth from where I lay in my sleeping-bag in the darkness was where Thérèse should have been. One minute I wanted to rage at her, to scream at her, and the next to start weeping.

I lay there wide awake and pictured her and Marshall touching, kissing, whispering to each other. I imagined myself stopping the flames and rekindling them at will, watching the fire blaze up into their faces, scorching into their flesh all the rage I felt. If I wanted, I could shout to them, I could rouse them to the danger they were in. Or I could look on, say nothing... and watch them burn.

I see Marshall blundering among the rubbish, his eyes streaming with the smoke and heat... He's stumbling towards the door, tugging at it. It won't budge. Coughing and retching, he staggers towards the shuttered back window.

The glass shatters, and there's a sudden roar as the fire sucks a rush of air into the blazing room.

Shouting and screaming in terror, he's driven back by the sudden flames. Back and further back to the door that's completely jammed. He starts clawing at the nearest wall, at the rotted plaster – his bare hands grasping and tearing at the wooden laths underneath, wrenching at them. Maddened by the heat, the choking smoke. Exhausted. Blinded almost, he's fallen to his knees, his fists are hammering at the openings he's gouged into the plaster and lathwork. Hammering until the blood runs from his knuckles – as if he could batter a way out through solid stonework.

I hear Thérèse's screams; her whole body's turned rigid

with terror. Her arms flung out, she's screaming for her life with all the force she's held inside until that final moment. No one will save her.

But even now, after all that has happened since then, I am in the room with her at the end, every time.

16

When I awoke the following morning, I was already in tears.

No matter where I went in Spain, Britain, anywhere in the world, I would never see Thérèse again. She no longer existed. Her sleeping-bag was lying flat. I touched the zipper, which she'd left half-open. I could remember almost nothing of our waking together that previous morning. The certainty that she herself had touched this fastener, that her living fingers had tugged at it to slide it down and never would again, overwhelmed everything else.

I reached forward to zip it shut, fold it up and put it away. In a few days or weeks I could return to Britain if I wanted to. I would put our time together behind me.

All those last weeks, while Thérèse and I had been shouting, swearing, screaming out loud as we ran through the woods, fighting and hurting each other and calling it love, she must still have been fucking that gnome. Love her? I'd hardly even known her. Not from when she'd first appeared as the rainbow-haired good-time girl come for a weekend at Les Montagnes Blanches had I ever known who she really was or what the hell was going on in her life. Her rainbow hair spread out on the pillow, on the grass or in the dirt, and the two of us going at each other with no holds barred – that was probably the most caring we'd been to each other. Towards the end, at least, there had been no pretence...

The fastener on her sleeping-bag was snagged. I tugged and tugged, but it just wouldn't give.

The way I was wrenching I'd be ripping the fucking thing apart any moment. I was on my knees with the open zip in one hand, the jammed fastener in the other and tugging at it for all I was worth. Probably at the very moment she'd slid the fastener down she'd been looking forward to her prearranged fuckers' tryst with Marshall. Had she been smiling when she climbed out of her sleeping-bag? I couldn't remember. Of course, I'd have thought she was smiling at me.

I bent forward to see where the material was catching and...

Her smell was suddenly all round me; the scent of her skin when she woke, the dry sweetness of her hair...

I made to throw the bag away but instead found that, all by themselves, my fingers were moving up and down the teeth of the open zip... like I was practising scales.

I'd been playing the piano when they brought my dad into the front room. There had been a ring at the door, my mother had answered it and a moment later his workmates were bearing him in. Though they carried him as gently as they could, I remember his crying out at every step. I stopped playing and went over to lift the bowl of dried flowers from the centre of the table to clear a space.

My first thought was shameful. Pure selfishness: I hoped that my dad wouldn't ask me to play for him while he lay there. I stood at the side of the table getting my excuses ready: he would need to rest, I'd suggest, he would need complete peace and quiet. As it was, my dad lay there the whole of the day, all the following night and...

The fucking zip wasn't going to give, no matter how hard I pulled. So let it stay like that. Who cared? Who the fuck cared?

I must have fallen asleep again, for it was much, much hotter, and the sea-green light coming through the tent wall had bleached to complete colourlessness when I heard Toni shouting for me: 'Jack! Jack!'

I sat up, stuck my head out of the tent. And stared.

There was no time to lose. On with the cleanest T-shirt, best jeans and trainers. I picked up Thérèse's rucksack and put it down again. Picked up her toilet bag, a French *policier* with a torn cover and her sleeping-bag, and put them down again.

Should I take her stuff with me or not? Better not. I could always return for it.

I paused. Took a deep breath.

I climbed out of the tent.

Thérèse's parents were waiting over by their car, Toni and Charlie beside them. It was a fifty-metre walk up to where they were standing. When Pablo and Claudine saw me coming, they turned away from Toni to look at me. To give me a good hard look. They didn't wave. They watched me approach every single step of the way.

It was Pablo who spoke first: 'So you are here.'

'Yes,' I managed, then stopped. I wanted to say how truly sorry I was, what a terrible thing had happened... But I could hardly get a word out.

'Yes,' I managed again, this time looking towards Claudine.

While the rest of her remained eyes front and stock-still, her lips made their reply: 'You will take us to... the place.' It was her voice, all right, but so very thin, so brittle.

The small stones rattled loosely and noisily as we stepped along the overgrown path in our three-abreast silence; our echoes coming back from the other side of the river gave a scale to the emptiness we were walking through.

A very long twenty minutes later, we arrived at the roofless, blackened-stone farmhouse. Near it, on the grass, were the sheets of corrugated iron we had dragged out, the lengths of scorched timber, broken tiles, twisted guttering, smashed window-frames, door panels...

Finally Pablo broke into speech: 'Here is it?'

I nodded.

Claudine wheeled round: 'Our daughter go away with you and come here. Now she is dead.'

Side by side they stared down at the burnt-out *finca*. Not a word was spoken.

At last, they about-turned and started marching back up the track. I followed a penitent dozen paces behind.

Claudine collected Thérèse's rucksack and sleeping-bag and put them in their car. Then she stood with her hand resting on the car roof and gazed out over the dried-up valley. Her face had hardened to a mask of unblinking eyes, pale unblemished skin and a mouth that was closed tight.

I approached her, but she did not bother to turn towards me. When she did speak, it was as if she were addressing the entire valley itself. 'My daughter did not come here. Thérèse was not here. No. Never.' She climbed into the car and pulled the door shut. She sat in the passenger seat, utterly rigid.

I held out to Pablo the blackened crescent-moon necklace that I'd been carrying around with me. 'This was her favourite necklace. Maybe Claudine might like to have it. You keep it until— ' I indicated Claudine ' —until you think the time is right.'

Pablo shook his head. Then, to my surprise, he tapped my hand, pushing the necklace back towards me. 'For you. It is best.' A moment's real contact between us.

Pablo went round to the driver's side of the car and climbed in.

There'd been no mention of the funeral arrangements they'd made and I didn't dare ask. They drove off along the track towards Buena Suerte without even once turning their heads for a final look.

Then they were gone.

There was no wind; the red dust from their car hung in the air, a smudged cloud above the track that would gradually clear, erasing their departure completely.

I was still staring after them when I heard someone come up behind me. I felt the touch of a hand on my arm.

'You OK, *amigo*?' It was Toni. 'You want coffee?'

I turned and hit him. As hard as I could, sending him sprawling back.

What the hell had I done that for?

'Jesus, Toni. I'm sorry, I'm sorry, I'm really sorry.' I reached out my hand and pulled him to his feet: 'It wasn't you, Toni, it wasn't anything. I don't...'

All at once I had to sit down. My whole body was trembling all over.

'I didn't mean to... I didn't mean to...' Whenever I started the sentence, the trembling would get worse.

I was staring down at the patch of colourless grass between my legs. Next thing, I was aware of someone sitting down beside me, putting their arms round me. I couldn't seem to stop shaking.

'You're a long way from home, sure enough.' Charlie's voice, though I hardly heard it above the mechanical rasp of insect noise, which, quite suddenly, seemed unbearably close up and almost deafening. Only then did I recognise what it had reminded me of that first day: the unending grind of my mother's sewing machine going day and night behind the closed front-room door, that relentless *prrrr*.

Charlie was stroking my hair now. I didn't try to speak any more. Let the stroking go on for ever as far as I was concerned, its kindness was so comforting, so soothing.

'Poor man.' I felt her lips press on to the top of my head – which almost made me burst into tears.

'Don't feel you have to leave us. You're welcome to stay.' She had begun to rock me backwards and forwards like a child.

'Yes, you want to stay – then you stay,' I heard Toni add.

She had started stroking and smoothing my hair again.

'Don't try to speak, Jack. Just rest. You're quite, quite worn out, and no real surprise at that.' Another light kiss. 'Rest, rest.'

Some time later I was being helped inside the shack, Charlie on one side, Toni on the other. A cooling breeze was blowing through the various cracks and loose window frames. They laid me down on their own bed.

I was aware of lying in a shaded place with, here and there, pinpoints of light marking the holes in the roof, and through the gaps between the planks that made up the walls longer shafts of light came slanting towards me. My eyes felt weighted, lead-heavy, and kept closing. Charlie was seated on the edge of the bed, holding my hand in hers. Now and again from outside I could hear the sounds of Toni moving about the yard. His subdued movements seemed to be coming from far away, and to come from a little further every time. My eyes had closed now and I could feel Charlie withdrawing her hand from mine. I didn't mind. I knew I was almost asleep.

It was dark when I awoke. I could hear the evening meal being prepared, the smell of woodsmoke. A long yawn, then a stretch.

'You have a good sleep? You feel better now?' Toni smiled at me as I stepped out of the doorway into the yard.

I smiled back. First things first, though. I went up the slope to go a few discreet steps further into the darkness.

I had just zipped up and was returning to the courtyard when I saw Rosa. She was sitting at the side of the woodstack. She didn't speak, but as I went by she reached out and offered me the joint she was smoking.

January 2004

1

It was noon, nearly a week or so after the fire. There was hardly a breath of air, just enough to make the sagging Martini umbrella shift slightly and its shadow pass backwards and forwards across the patch of beaten earth at my feet. I stared out at the unfinished sheds and walls of Paradise, and beyond them to the river. The heat haze made the whole scene unreal, something I couldn't quite believe in. The chair I was sitting on didn't seem solid, nor did the cabin behind me, nor the trees, the clumps of cacti, the scrub, the stones, not even the red earth at my feet.

I drank my tea, ate my lunchtime tinned frankfurters and maize while a thousand-strong squadron of insects buzzed and whined about the plate. The skin on the lower part of my arm was deeply tanned, not brown-black, but soon would be. Behind me, Rosa's cabin gave off a blistering heat I could feel raking my back.

'If that bitch had not come here...' For the third time in as many days, Rosa was telling me the story of the fire.

I took a sip of coffee and gazed out at the valley. Spreading to an invisibility far in the distance, everything appeared as if remembered from a dream. As usual, I had hardly slept the night before, and now I felt I was trespassing on a day that, for me, hadn't quite begun.

'...they say to go to church for Marshall in Barcelona. I am angry at him, yes. But I go. Now I feel is good I go. Now everything finished.' Rosa leaned back in her chair, wiped the sweat and stray maize from her upper lip, then flicked away the last scrap of onion. Together we watched the slice of oiled translucence arc itself greasily in the noonday brightness and fall on the dried ground.

Immediately, I pictured Thérèse's shiny crescent pendant. Two days after the fire, when the others went to the church service for Marshall, I had gone alone to the burned-out *finca* and nailed the silver necklace to the charred remains of the mantelpiece jutting out from the stonework. There it hung freely – a shrine, of sorts. I couldn't think what else to do with it. Sometimes, like now, I pictured the silver crescent hanging there, swaying backwards and forwards in the slight breeze. It was comforting, almost.

Rosa had just said something: 'Is really good that you help me, Jack. *Muchas gracias*. If you do not help, then I cannot do anything. Without you, I must go away and must leave Paradise.'

I nodded.

She was looking directly at me. 'Is really kind that you do this. I know you not like me.'

I said nothing.

'It is true. No?'

An ant was already tugging at the fallen half-moon of onion while a few more marched up to help. I turned to face her. 'I wouldn't say that.'

'I say it for you.' It was the first time I had ever seen Rosa smile.

I shrugged.

She went on: 'Your bitch was problem for everyone. If your bitch not come here, then Marshall not dead.' Then she added: 'You kill them?'

'What?' I stared at her.

'You kill them, Jack? I will tell no one, I promise. No police, no one.' She leaned towards me: '*Por favor*, I want to hear.'

I looked away. 'It was an accident, wasn't it? They fell asleep – Marshall's cigarette. Like you told the police, like you keep telling me.'

'Yes, Jack, I know this – but it make no sense. Not possible. Why do they not leave? The bad smoke makes them want to leave, no? They wake, they— ' she made a coughing noise 'they get frightened, they break the door, the window. They leave. No?'

I stood up. 'Thanks for the food, Rosa. It's time I was getting back to— '

'No key there. You understand? Door was fixed shut. Someone fix this. That someone is you, Jack?'

'Sounds like *you're* the one who's got it all thought out.'

'*Perdón?* What you say?'

'Maybe it was you who fixed everything, maybe it was you who— '

She jumped to her feet. 'NO! Never. No! I try help them. I try *rescue* them. I not love Marshall, but I not burn him dead – not him and not your bitch.'

'You didn't love him? Why were you staying with him?'

'Life not so simple, not anywhere – and not here.'

We were standing facing each other. The slight breeze had dropped to nothing. I hadn't murdered them, and she said she hadn't. OK, end of story.

'I am very sorry I make you angry.' She took a step towards me. 'I want to know, Jack, to *know*, that is all. Not to tell. But maybe to know everything – is not possible. Maybe we never know. Maybe we never understand.' She placed her hand lightly on my shoulder. 'You and me, Jack, we not understand what happen – but we work, we help each other. That is important – no?'

She was looking closely into my face.

'Rosa, I…' But I wasn't sure how to reply.

'Wait, please. I want you know the real Marshall – what he really like.'

Before I could stop her, she had lifted her arms and begun taking off her T-shirt. She let it drop to the ground. Then, without pausing, she undid her shorts, let them fall and stepped out of them, kicking off her sandals at the same time. She stood in front of me quite naked. Slowly she began to turn round.

I couldn't hold back a sharp catch of breath: parts of her back, from shoulder to thigh, were marked blue-black with bruises. Much, much worse than when I saw her that first time.

'These he leave me. In the last days he is very… *Bueno*, you see.'

'Jesus Christ!'

She turned round to face me again. 'In time it will be OK, I know this.'

She took my hand and laid it on to a half-healed cut just below her right shoulder, the scab felt ridged and hardened.

Without letting go, she took my other hand and made me touch a bruise on her right hip.

'*Sí*, but now it is very much pain. Sometimes it feel like a dead man's hands touch me.' As she said this, her gaze had gone far out into the early afternoon.

'I'm very sorry, Rosa. It's terrible how Marshall died, but you're much better off now. Without him, without all this.'

'And you, Jack? How you feel? No, do not move away your hands, please. Is comfort. They soothe a little. For you, I think it is more terrible, more difficult... to be without her. I know that you in love.'

Just then, a bit of remembered therapy-speak popped into my mind. It seemed to fit the bill. 'Yes, Rosa, I hurt too. But for me the pain is on the inside.' Then I paused.

I started rehearsing to myself some suitable phrases to get us beyond where we were, without any awkwardness: a few words touching on the sadness we'd shared and expressing the hope that we would, each in our own way, find the strength to go on with our lives. I polished the phrases over in my mind, simplifying them so she would understand – even trying to remember some words in Spanish: words like *sadness, hope, strength, independence*. Meanwhile, I breathed in the earthy sweat of her hair and felt the roughness of her wounded skin.

I paused too long.

'*Sí*, Jack, I think that I understand. I am sorry that I have no help for you. I am very, very sorry.' She lifted one of my hands to her lips. I could feel the warmth of her breath against my skin. She didn't kiss me, just drew her mouth very lightly along one of the fingers. 'My back too? You comfort? Please?'

Compassion? Cowardice? I couldn't just walk away and leave her standing there like that. I could already imagine her broken skin flinching when I touched it, and so my hand was shaking as I raised it up to her shoulder.

There was an intake of breath. 'Please, more. It feel good. Very good. Please, for more time. *Sí, sí*. It is good comfort.'

A few moments later, she had begun breathing more deeply.

'*Sí*, it feel so good, so good.'

Under my fingers, I could feel the tension in her body easing little by little. Maybe at last I was actually doing someone some good, if only for a short time. This could very well be the woman who'd burned Thérèse to death and who'd burned her own man to death, I told myself. But my hands had taken on a life of their own. A moment of tenderness, of compassion even.

Finally we stepped apart. In silence, I brushed my fingers lightly down the side of her face, leaving a smear on the sweat and dirt on her cheek. It felt like a benediction.

I let my hands fall to my side.

'We should get back to work.'

Rosa said nothing. She gave a nod and pulled on her clothes.

Five minutes later we were standing side by side next to a stack of breeze blocks, slapping on the cement. What else was there to do?

It was while I was finishing off the gap round the window frame that I suddenly thought of my mother. Could she possibly have heard about the fire and be worried? Only an outside chance, of course, but to be on the safe side I decided to send her a card wishing her a late but very happy new year.

I'd mention the fire in a PS, reassuring her that I'd been nowhere near the place and was fine.

Problem solved. I smiled to myself and ladled on another trowelful of cement.

2

Yes, Mr FixIt was well and truly back in business carrying on precisely where Marshall had left off, only much more efficiently. Forget the crazy man's Five-Year Plan of equal development on all fronts; at my suggestion we stuck to working on one building, the main shed. Together, Rosa and I hammered, sawed and cemented until we were exhausted. Apart from her obsession with the fire story, we talked only about cement, breeze blocks and wood. Nothing else. No more thinking, no more remembering. We were sleepwalkers shambling through an unfinished dream.

Our day's work done, she'd ask me to lay my hands on her scars for *comfort*. We'd share a trough of heated-up chilli con carne or tinned ham with beans. Leaving her alone to sit listening to her battery-powered radio, I'd slog the eight hundred metres back to Toni and Charlie's. A few joints would get rolled, then a few more. Afterwards I'd feel my way in the darkness to the tent, where I'd fall, quite literally, asleep.

At night Thérèse came to me, her skin blackened and scorched, her hair in flames.

Then I would wake up screaming. And remain wide awake for the rest of the night.

Hours later I would drag myself out of my sleeping-bag, out of the tent. One step at a time, I'd force myself back down the track to get through another day. And then through the day after that.

I worked myself into complete exhaustion to help Rosa. Kindness, or a kind of penance? I knew that the longer I stayed the harder it would be to leave. But so far I hadn't left. I seemed unable to pull myself together to make the effort. One day just seemed to lead to the next, and to the next after that...

One evening, about three weeks after the fire, I'd no sooner hauled myself back through the falling darkness into Toni and Charlie's when I was offered a mug of red wine and an unexpected portion of *jamón montaña* with white asparagus – a celebratory feast, they explained. I knew Charlie had been teaching that day; afterwards she would have stocked up on supplies as usual – but exotic ham and asparagus? I glanced round to see what was up for celebration. Had the leaks been mended? Unlikely, considering the number of pots, pans and pails scattered round. Had the windows been properly screwed in? There seemed to be as much fresh air and insects circulating as ever. So what was it? I waited by the light of the paraffin lamp and the hiss of a thousand mosquitoes while the two of them grinned at me.

Finally Toni refilled our mugs for a toast and made the official announcement: Charlie was pregnant.

A drawing-in of breath, an enthusiastic whoop of delight, then congratulations, handshaking, back-slapping and, in the absence of cigars, fresh joints all round.

Announcement number two came a moment later: they'd

be leaving for Barcelona some time in the next few weeks. Their shack, they added, was mine. If I wanted it.

One final thing, they almost forgot: a letter had come for me. They'd picked it up in Buena Suerte. I recognised the handwriting immediately. My mother must have given her the address.

I ripped it open.

Happy Birthday!
How are you?
Anna

3

The following morning I headed down the track, one leaden foot after the other. I wasn't carrying anything, yet by the time I arrived at Paradise I felt completely exhausted – and would probably feel so for the rest of the day.

Anna. Poor Anna. How was I? she'd asked. Difficult answering that on the back of a postcard. Not that I intended trying. One glance at her handwriting had taken me straight back to the Gare du Nord. Guilt, like a rush of ice-cold water over me. Guilt, like a blade twisting inside. She'd even remembered my birthday – which was more than I had. There was a lizard watching me from where it was sunning itself on a nearby stone. I stepped closer for a better look – instantly, it tail-flicked itself from sight. I walked on.

Rosa had her back to me as I came walking down the track. She was naked and giving herself a shower. The water, pumped up from the river, could be diverted directly into a sprinkler fixed to a pole; showers were effortless and lasted longer than a bucketful. *Chez* Rosa, living standards were the best in the valley. Bottled gas powered a cooking-ring, a gaslight and even a small fridge. As she sluiced and sponged I could see that her welts and bruises were well on the mend.

At the sound of my footsteps in the dirt yard she jerked round, the water still dripping from her face. Seeing it was me, she relaxed. 'You want coffee?'

The daily furnace was getting itself turned up to 'Continental warm' – which really meant 'Scottish hot'. A new generation of biters and whiners was already test-flying, and a strongish wind was catching its breath with a few practice gusts before letting rip. Over by the shed we'd been working on, a torn plastic sack scraped to and fro against a tumbled heap of breeze blocks. Having filled the mugs and covered them with old saucers, I looked out at what the day had to offer.

Today we planned to put in windows. Professional builders finish their building first, then position and secure the frames in the precisely measured gaps left to accommodate them. Being strictly amateur, I intended to slot in the windows as and where they were required, then carry on building the rest of the walls round them. Any fine and not-so-fine adjustments would be made with a hammer and chisel, any mistakes covered by a cosmetic slap-on of extra cement.

After she'd slipped into the cement-stiffened shirt and hacked-off-at-the-knees jeans, Rosa joined me at the cold-buffet breakfast: last night's leftovers with a grated cheese topping, fuel rather than food.

'Today *un poco frío*. Not hot. Better for work, no?' She was having a biscuit for afters.

Breakfast over, she got to her feet, wandered off behind the cabin, then came back fastening her jeans on the way.

Two hours later we'd reached the stage of positioning the first window. We took an end each of the wooden frame and lifted. Thanks to the blustery conditions, the sheet of glass became all corners and awkwardness, like a filled sail blowing us in every direction. We made a real Laurel and Hardy job of it, tugging, dropping and smashing two of them before we got the third slotted in. Next came the sensitive craftsman bit: nails at each corner and bucketfuls of cement. Job done. Once the cement hardened, I could lard on another bucketful for that smooth professional finish.

It was now gusting strongly, a bone-dry, searing cut of a wind. From time to time, usually when trying to get the sweat out of my eyes, I'd tip my trowel that critical tip too far. Not that it mattered: any cement that slopped on to Rosa was shrugged off without comment. There was never much small talk. I'd been blinking my eyes for the hundredth time in the last hour to clear them of sweat and dirt when I heard my name called, and Rosa's.

I looked up – and there, coming hand in hand along the track towards us, were a very clean Toni and a very clean Charlie. Even at twenty metres they seemed to glow in the late-morning sun. Toni had shaved, and Charlie was wearing her best teaching clothes.

Greetings exchanged, the explanations followed.

After the previous night's celebration they'd woken up thinking they'd have to leave at some point soon, so why not now? Having turned Tombo and Evie loose to rejoin the other horses, they'd decided on a last farewell walk through the countryside to the road end. There was a bus leaving Buena Suerte in the afternoon, and they intended to be on it.

They gave us an address in Valencia – Toni's family apparently – and promised to write. If I wanted it, their shack was now all mine. There were some kitchen things, a couple of spades, a few boxes of candles, mosquito coils, matches and the like, as well as the rest of the supplies they'd brought back the day before. Also, there was some grass needing to be smoked and veg needing to be picked.

Toni looked ten years younger; Charlie looked excited. When they came visiting next year to show us their first born, she grinned, would the place be finished by then? We laughed and promised to start on the guest wing.

We said goodbye and watched them walk back to where their rucksacks lay at the top of the track. The wind that seemed to have died down for a moment now picked up again even more strongly. As they turned, I could see Charlie's red hair being lifted and swept across her face. One last wave, and they were gone.

I stared after them.

What about me? What would I do now? Days toiling in the sun? Nights lying in the darkness, in that cockroach-ridden shambles of a shack? Was that it?

I was within a touch of dropping tools there and then, scarpering back to the tent, grabbing my rucksack and rushing along the track to catch up with them. No more Rosa, no more Paradise.

Instead, I looked on while my hand slapped another trowelful of wet cement on to the top layer of bricks...

An hour later it was time for a break. I downed tools and went over to slump into the shade under the umbrella.

We ate in silence. We finished. I was getting myself ready to stretch out on the ground for a siesta when Rosa came over to me: 'I have something for you, Jack, if you want. Something special,' she said almost shyly. 'Come, I show you.'

The sun lay like a sheet of hot metal across my shoulders as I followed her up the steps into the cabin.

4

She hadn't washed, but then neither had I. Having stripped off her T-shirt and shorts, she gave herself a quick wipe-over with a towel.

Naked, she lay face down on the bed. 'Please, I need comfort.'

Because the wind was sending the dirt and dust whirling about the room, I closed the door behind me. Immediately the temperature rose ten degrees. I stepped round a pile of clothes tangled on the floor.

In the discoloured light seeping through the grime-caked window, it was difficult to see her skin very clearly, to distinguish between shadows and bruising. I leaned over her and placed my hands on her back ready to begin smoothing away the last signs of cruelty.

When my ritual act of healing was almost completed, she turned over and looked up at me. Her face was cement-streaked where she'd rubbed the sweat from her eyes and cheeks.

We didn't speak.

When I had finished, she reached up to lay her hand on my arm. Immediately a pool of sweat formed where our skin touched.

'Jack?'

She slid her hand up my arm.

'Jack, please.'

I said nothing. I didn't move.

She began pulling me towards her.

'Please.'

It seemed hotter than ever. With my free hand I brushed the sweat from my eyes, but it was replaced immediately by more sweat. I was dripping onto her, but she didn't seem to notice or to care.

'Some good time is all.' She was looking straight into my face, not smiling. 'Everyone need some good time. You need? You want?' Then she added: 'Please.'

When I got up from the bed afterwards, she was lying quietly. From the doorway I called back: 'See you later.'

'*Sí*, later. A little siesta.'

Though it was mid-afternoon and the hottest time of the day, I walked all the way down to the river and lowered myself into the remaining shallows of the bathing pool. After splashing myself to get rid of the caked dirt and cement I returned to the bank. Now what? Back to Rosa's?

The door of her cabin was still shut. Not that I could imagine going back into that closed and stifling room. Was she hoping I would become another Marshall, Marshall Mark Two – the gentle version?

What the hell was I going to do? And as for that birthday card from Anna... Her few words seemed to have come from another life, from another world altogether.

So what kind of life was this?

I skirted the edge of Paradise and set off up the track to what was now my very own place in the sun. My very own shack.

Toni and Charlie had certainly left in a hurry.

The place had always looked a mess, but now it looked like an abandoned mess. Clothes were lying everywhere, cardboard boxes had been torn and thrown aside, an old tea chest was split open. I trampled across a litter of books, playing cards, chess pieces, tools, saw blades, lengths of rope, candle stubs, discarded batteries and other rubbish. When I reached the bed I threw myself on to the mattress and closed my eyes.

What the hell was I doing here?

I opened my eyes and glanced round at the mess and confusion. I should get up, take what was mine and leave. Simple as that.

My eyes closed again.

The noise of an engine woke me. I remained perfectly still.

The engine was switched off.

A moment later there was a rap on the door. Of course, I could always pretend not to be there – but Rosa would then have walked straight in. I got up and went to answer it.

5

Her hair seemed longer than before, and slightly darker. Had she dyed it a little? Were streaks of it tinted maybe? Or wasn't I remembering properly? It was over six months since I'd abandoned her at the Gare du Nord.

She was carrying a shoulder bag. She gave a hesitant smile. 'Long time no see.'

'Anna!... Hello.'

Meanwhile I was wondering to myself: blondes usually stay blonde – so why the change? And as for letting it grow longer...?

Was that all I could think about? Her new hairstyle?

We were standing out in the yard, in the full sun. Round us, the insects were droning and whining. Somewhere to my left an invisible bird called out *gach-gach* from within the thick dark leaves of a fig tree. I could feel the sweat running down my back.

We kissed, lightly on each cheek. Continental style.

This was the moment to take a step back, and offer her some water or beer. Then say I was pleased to see her.

We sat in the courtyard shade, side by side in the leather car seats, with our backs against the woodpile, a bottle of beer each. Anna told me about how she'd asked the driver to wait for ten minutes – and if she didn't come back out of the shack, he was free to return to Buena Suerte.

'I had to pay him extra for that – just as well you're pleased to see me!' Then came a look of accusation: 'You are pleased – aren't you?'

Before I could answer, the words started tumbling out of her: 'Did you know that the Edinburgh Hogmanay party was cancelled this year – at the very last minute? Because of the bad weather, they said. Terrorist threat, more likely. A cell full of them were arrested in Leith last year, remember?'

She took a sip of her beer. 'I got really pissed, lost the bunch of friends I'd gone out with, wandered up and down Princes Street with the other drunks, the police and the street cleaners. Sat down on the steps of the RSA gallery, started crying and couldn't seem to stop. I felt so angry and helpless, so enraged and betrayed, utterly desolate and alone. End-of-the-year blues doesn't even begin to describe it...' She managed a half-smile. 'I saw your address when you wrote to your mum, so I sent you the birthday card. Later on I thought: the world's coming to an end, we'll all get blown up any minute, and that's my best shot – *a birthday card*?'

She finished her drink and looked me full in the face. 'So here I am!'

Not quite managing to say the words *I'm very pleased you've come*, I raised my beer. 'Cheers.'

We clinked bottles. I gave her an edited version of life in the valley. Told her about Marshall and the fire, about Toni and Charlie leaving and that the shack was now officially mine. I was a man of property.

Then came the interrogation.

How did I come to be here in the first place?

I gave her a vague reply about meeting a friend of Toni's in Paris.

What did I do all day?

I helped Rosa in Paradise. The poor woman had just lost her husband. I explained that I stayed in the tent, which she must have passed when walking down from the track. I pointed in its direction, as though offering proof of something. About Thérèse I didn't say a word. It seemed the most tactful thing to do.

'You're living here quite alone?'

'Oh, yes.'

For several moments we sat without speaking, staring out into the sun-bleached, empty landscape.

She turned to me. 'It was a long trip. So where's the bathroom?'

At dinner that evening, under a sky of falling stars, she told me the real reason she had come: she was pregnant.

I had been about to dish out the vegetables. A spoonful of courgette was arrested in mid-air. I let it fall back into the pot.

Without knowing why, I thought first of Rosa: that sad, bruised woman only a fifteen-minute walk away through the darkness. Sitting on one of the canvas picnic seats, with only her radio and the smoke of her mosquito coil for company. Behind her, the rubbish tip of a cabin with the plans for Paradise still nailed to the wall. Was she wondering if I'd show up next morning as usual?

I dragged my mind back to Anna.

Pregnant. Jesus.

She was saying something. 'At least you've not rushed off.'

'No.' Then, before I could stop myself, I added: 'Where's there to rush to?'

Anna had poured two glasses of red from the nearly full wine box that Toni and Charlie had left behind. 'We may as well toast the happy event.' She clinked her glass against mine, which I'd not yet picked up. 'Not that I'm supposed to be drinking, of course. Cheers!'

'Cheers!'

We drank.

She sat with the glass cradled in her hands. 'I could have

got rid of it. Got myself scraped out. No problem.'

I nodded.

'But I didn't. Nobody knows. Except you now. The lucky father.'

Though her voice had sounded steady and she hadn't moved, I could see tears running down her face.

I leaned towards her. 'Anna...'

'Don't say a word, Jack.' She took a deep breath. 'Like I said, I wanted to get rid of it. Believe me. Knowing it was yours, I really wanted to. I was more alone than you could ever imagine.'

'But your foster parents...'

'Foster parents, set number three,' she hissed. 'You never met them – or you wouldn't even think to mention— ' she choked back a sob ' —to mention them.' Another sob. 'But there was your mother, Jack. I was calling to see her every fortnight or so. Each time I pressed the bell, I said to myself: this time I'll tell her. She'll be a grandmother; it'll bring us all together. Each time I visited I wanted to tell her. And I didn't. She talked about you. Made excuses for you. About how you used to play the piano, how you won prizes. A sensitive boy, she said. Sensitive! Jesus!'

She finished her wine, then refilled her glass. Inside me, the same phrase kept repeating itself over: *a father; you're going to be a father.*

She leaned forward to take another sip of wine, but instead replaced the glass untouched and continued speaking.

'When I got to Buena Suerte, I asked them in the shop. That's how I knew where to come.' She gazed round the yard, the sagging woodpile, the makeshift tarpaulin veranda, the unconnected cooker, the paraffin lamp, the mess everywhere, the mosquitoes whining round our heads. Finally, letting her glance remain on me for several seconds, she said, 'What a dump it is, though.'

This time she raised her glass, draining nearly all of it in one. She wiped the tears from her face. 'So, Jack, here we are.'

For a split second I felt we had been set there, posed by some unknown photographer who was waiting nearby in the darkness, camera raised and focused to catch this scene of domestic togetherness. If I moved even slightly, I would make the picture blur. I would spoil it.

'Jack?'

'I'm… I'm pleased you're here.'

I was very surprised to hear myself, but I seemed to be saying the right words. They felt unfamiliar but right. Or maybe I was just feeling my way forwards and, in time, these unlikely words would indeed come to express what I was feeling. Maybe.

'Pleased for me? For us?'

'I'm glad you didn't… didn't terminate.'

'I'm not. Like I said, I really wanted to. Wanted to get you and everything about you out of my life, and out of me. But I just couldn't.' She shrugged. 'You really hurt me, you bastard! You fucking bastard! When I realised you'd run off, abandoning me on that train… it was the worst moment of my life… the very fucking worst.

'For fuck's sake, Jack, I don't *want* to be pregnant. I don't really know what I want any more. Maybe I don't even want to be here. Not really. Who knows? But here I am.'

We began to eat. The food had gone cold.

*

Later, once we'd shaken the mattress for wrigglies and biters, we lay side by side in our separate sleeping-bags. The mosquitoes whined round us in the darkness.

'How can you live in this... this squalor? How?'

It took me several seconds to reply. This time I knew I was telling the truth. 'I don't know.'

She laughed. 'You don't know what you're doing here and I don't know what the hell I'm doing here either – but here we are, the pair of us. Maybe we really do belong together. How does that grab you?'

Instead of answering, I reached across to place my hand on her sleeping-bag, guessing where her belly would be. 'Is that where... ?'

'Somewhere around there, Jack, yes.'

I nodded in the darkness.

6

When I awoke next morning, I lay staring up at the gaps in the roof. They were now my very own gaps, in my very own roof. That could be my job for the day. That, and adjusting to prospective fatherhood. Funny thing was – Anna didn't *look* pregnant. At six months and a bit, surely something would have to show? Or maybe not? Wouldn't she be sick first thing when she woke up? I was pretty hazy on the details.

Then again, she could easily go and pretend to be sick.

As I gazed straight up I could understand why Toni had placed the bed at such an odd angle to the wall – directly above me was a stretch of roof with no scraps of blue sky showing through. Though the rest of the valley might be drenched in a sudden Continental downpour, so long as I didn't move the bed to the left, or to the right, but kept it under that miraculous section of corrugated iron, I alone would remain dry. My bed, my very own raft in a drowning world.

Time to slip off for a quick pee...

'Not leaving me again, are you?' The old Anna was peering out at me through the eyes of the new. Then came a smile. 'I suppose you could say the bathroom here really is *en suite*. Takes up the rest of the valley.'

'Back in a minute. Promise.'

I picked my way down the path between the fig and almond trees. As if I were some kind of malign spirit, the racket from the insects turned to silence the instant I approached. Standing on a low rise, I peed into the dry dust at my feet. Waves of heat came rolling across the valley, turning the scene into an out-of-focus photograph already losing colour. A disturbance to my right made me glance down towards the river. Two of the horses were standing there. I could hear them snorting and tossing their manes, their front hooves pawing at the loose stones on the river bed.

Anna was waiting for me when I returned.

'Finding some clean towels for me, were you?' Was this the old Anna or the new?

'No, I was— '

'It's OK, Jack. Just kidding!'

I managed a smile.

'But you do have more than one towel here?'

'Oh, yes.'

'There's a certain happiness that's measured only in fluffy clean towels – and I don't mean that therapeutically!'

Smile number two. So, no morning sickness.

We spent the next couple of hours walking about the nearby countryside, a guided excursion that skirted the barbed-wire boundary of Paradise. The Toyota stood parked at the side of the cabin. Thankfully, there was no sign of Rosa.

'That's the place I was telling you about – where Marshall used to live and where I sometimes go to give his widow a hand.'

'That all you give her?' Anna laughed. It seemed she'd been making another joke.

Enough said.

As we walked along, we picked and ate figs; we watched lizards; we listened to birds; we managed a very shallow paddle in the river. When a few horses showed up to drink, I pointed out Tombo and Evie.

The last stop on the guided tour was a request one: Anna's request, not mine. From where we stood on the track above, the interior of the *finca* was clearly visible between the burned-out spars of the roof. It was like a building plan that had been scribbled over: we could see where the cooking stove belonged, and which spaces were for windows, doorways, the kitchen recess. In the back room a blackened heap sagged against the wall like a burst-open refuse sack – this was all that remained of the mattress. *Their* mattress.

'If the place was so derelict, what was the man, Marshall, doing here?'

I explained that he'd probably been salvaging wood and

roof tiles for his own building work. For that extra touch of authenticity I gave her an extended version of the Marshall-falling-asleep-while-he-was-smoking theory.

'Let's have a look round.' She started down the slope.

'Careful,' I shouted after her, 'the floor's dangerous...'

But she'd already stepped through the gap where the door used to be. All I could think was: *If she sees Thérèse's pendant hanging up in there, turning slowly on its silver chain, catching the light...*

'It's not too bad,' she called back.

I knew what I should do: casually walk in, take up the Marshall chat where I'd left off, developing the theme and adding that it was lucky he hadn't set the whole valley on fire – to illustrate my point I'd indicate the window and the tinder-dry conditions outside. Then, having successfully distracted Anna's attention, I'd snatch the pendant.

She zigzagged her way across the room, carefully keeping to the floor joists that now spanned the earth-pit below. Since a section of the floor had completely given way under its weight, part of the upended piano now stuck above floor level, angled upwards like a boat in the act of sinking.

'Someone's pride and joy that must have been.'

'Yes, a real shame.' Meanwhile, I edged nearer the mantel-piece where I could see the silver crescent moon hanging on its chain, fortunately partly in shadow. 'Yes, Marshall was always smoking. Rolled his own. He— '

'What's that?'

She was pointing right at the pendant.

'What?'

'That – hanging over there. Like a key or something.'

'It's... It's... I'll check it out.' Two steps would take me there. Two steps, and then Anna would ask to see it, to hold it. She would recognise it...

I took the first step.

'Oh, Christ! Look, Jack, up in the rafters!'

I looked. At first I didn't see what she was so excited about. Then *it* moved. It slithered.

Next thing, Anna had turned and fled.

Leaving the pendant for the moment, I followed her outside. She was sitting on the ground, looking rather pale.

'I got a fright, that was all. A beautiful snake, though. So sleek.'

I saw my chance. 'Some snakes can be dangerous, like that one, I think. Better safe than sorry.'

Danger over, she got to her feet. 'The government health warnings are true, then: smoking kills.'

'Anna!' I really was shocked. 'That's a bit much. The poor guy— '

'Therapeutically speaking, of course, the certainty of death is always with us.' Then she rubbed her hand over her stomach and gave me a smile. 'It is the promise of new life which is the real miracle.' After a pause, she added: 'I know we're going to make it, Jack. This time.'

As we began to leave, she took my arm. I resumed tour-guide mode. 'That's the local sights, pretty much. Back to the shack for a spot of lunch?'

'Then we'll talk.'

We walked the next few steps in silence.

'You know what I mean, Jack – *talk*. Talk about what we're doing. About what we're going to do.'

'Right.'

'Our future, Jack, is in our own hands.'

After a pause to respect the therapeutic gravity of her statement, I replied: 'Of course.'

'You do want a future, don't you?'

'Eh? Of course I do. That's a funny question.'

She came to an abrupt halt and looked me full in the face. 'Not so very funny, Jack, not really. In fact, it is the most important question I know. And it is a question I ask myself every single day of my life – and every single day I try to answer it with a "yes".'

'Oh.'

We continued walking.

7

Side by side the two of us strolled through the perfect noonday stillness. A cloudless blue sky, not a breath of wind. Every bush, every patch of scrub seemed outlined to a sharpness honed by sunlight. The only sounds were the scuff of occasional loose stones under our feet and the crackle of brittle-dry grass. I made a note to return and remove Thérèse's pendant another time. Which I've now done – not that it matters any more.

We walked back along the path to the shack without speaking – a couple of casually sketched-in figures drifting across a precisely painted landscape. Ahead of us, as I was soon to discover, the vanishing point of the composition was already in place.

'I have to stop.'

Anna had stepped into the shade of a large tree. Looking

out at me, she seemed all that remained alive in this dying landscape of primary colours. 'You go on if you want, Jack. You can pick the cockroaches out of the bed for me and have some water ready. It's not far, is it?'

'No, about five minutes.'

'Might as well be five hours. I've got to rest.'

'Take your time, just follow this path. When you get up the slope, you'll see the shack. Not far, really.'

'Just make the bed habitable.'

I gave her a wave and walked off, my steps suddenly much lighter. This was the first time I had been by myself since she arrived. The first time I'd had a chance to think. I marched along, trying my hardest to concentrate: left-right/left-right/left-right... I tried and tried, but could get no further than Anna here/Anna pregnant/Anna here/Anna pregnant...

I turned into the yard. Ahead of me, in the dimness under the tarpaulin shade, I saw movement. Someone was standing there.

'*Hola*, Jack!' It was Rosa. She looked fresher and cleaner than usual with her hair washed and tied back, yellow T-shirt, her smartest jeans and trainers. All dressed for a social call.

'Hello, Rosa. I was going to come to— '

'No, Jack. I understand. Yesterday was very wrong. I was too sad. *Muy triste, muy dolorosa*. Everything was too sad. And I needed... I needed...' She shrugged. 'But not again. I come to say that I am sorry. I come to say that what happen, what we... I come to say that it not happen again... Never happen again. *Entiende?*'

I was only half-listening. At any moment Anna would be turning up.

'... Today I go to Vic. If you want, Jack, please, you come

too. Together we have holiday. We have *fiesta*. Good food, good wine to say again sorry and that we are friends. Not every day work.' She paused and smiled at me. 'Please? You want?'

'Well... ' I began, then saw she wasn't listening. She was looking beyond me now and had seen something. Seen *someone*. Her smile faded.

'OK, Jack. I understand why you not come for work this morning. I will go.' She touched me lightly on the arm. '*Hasta la vista*.' Then she hurried off.

Shortly afterwards, Anna was indoors stretched out on the bed and I was in the yard, crouched down blowing a handful of twigs into flame under the cooker grill. Normal life had resumed.

There was a light tap on my shoulder. I turned.

'What— ?'

Rosa stood there, her finger to her lips for silence. She beckoned me to follow her a few metres up the path.

'I think maybe I leave Paradise. I go visit friends in Tarragona. Talk to them, and think. You stay in Paradise, you... and friend.'

'She just appeared out of nowhere. Yesterday afternoon. Anna is an old friend from Scotland. We don't really know what we're— '

'*No importante*. Stay if you want. Go if you want. Or you want live here in this camping mess of Toni? Better to live in Paradise. Roof is good, no *cucaracha* in bed, you and friend eat chilli con carne, frankfurter. You keep out *serpiente* for me, *sí*? Maybe I come back soon, maybe never.'

After a few seconds I said: 'Rosa, I am really sorry.'

'Sorry – yes. I too very sorry. I go visit my Tarragona

friends and…' But she didn't move away.

'Good luck anyway, Rosa.' When I reached forward to kiss her once on each cheek, she put her arms round me and held me close.

'Not you I leave, but everything I leave. All the years – everything. *Adiós*.'

Then she broke free, turned and walked away without looking back.

Going indoors a short time later with a mug of tea for Anna, I found her fast asleep. I was glad not to have to talk to her.

Before dinner that evening we walked to the beginning of the track leading down to Rosa's – the Toyota was gone.

That night we slept in Paradise.

8

Rosa had made a half-hearted attempt to tidy up the cabin for us. Most of the junk had been pushed against one wall, which made the place look bigger. The grimy sheets had been changed and the bed freshly made up. The small table had been cleared, and on it stood a gift: nestling in an inviting semicircle of tinned chilli con carne, with more tins stacked on top, was her little battery radio. Perhaps, returning to the outside world, she felt she no longer needed it. The right-hand corner of the neat plan of Paradise was missing – the stick figures had been torn off.

After a starlit meal of frankfurters and mixed veg, we switched on the radio for some background music to our after-dinner conversation. When the music stopped, an announcer started speaking. Some of what he said was clear enough – even to us.

Guerra, Iraq, Americanos, muerte...

'Switch it off, Jack.'

'I keep forgetting we're in Spain... '

'No, we're in Paradise!' Anna was slightly stoned.

Baghdad, bomba, violencia, terrorismo...

'Switch it off. We're on our Paradise holiday. A family Paradise holiday – until we decide what kind of family we are. We'll soon have to think of our baby, remember. We'll have to talk and make plans – not just do what suits us any more.'

The bed was wriggly-proof: each leg stood in a small tin of water to repel the ants, cockroaches and other crawlers. It felt like being in an upside-down castle with its towers set in four puddle-moats, a refuge of sorts.

About a week after Anna's arrival, while taking a rest from pumping out a dribble of water for washing, I found myself staring blankly down at the parched ground at my feet, at the meaningless pattern of cracks that covered the dried-up earth. That was when it suddenly occurred to me: her birthday card had arrived well after the farmhouse had burned down – *but wasn't it possible that Anna herself had set the fire?*

After all, she had told me about her terrible time on Hogmanay – her helpless rage and sense of complete abandonment now that she was pregnant. No doubt my mum had mentioned Buena Suerte to her at some point – once she'd flown to Barcelona, making her way to the small village and asking around for Toni's place would have been easy enough. Perhaps she arrived just in time to catch sight of Thérèse going into the farmhouse? Seeing *Thérèse* – what a total shock that would have been! I'd never once mentioned Thérèse to my mother. Anna would have been devastated. Devastated – and enraged. Within seconds, her devastation has turned to utter fury. She and her unborn child have come all the way from Britain – for *this*? So she jams the door shut and sets the place on fire. She returns to Edinburgh. Later, she visits my mum again and learns I'd been nowhere near the farmhouse at the time and was still very much alive. So, with her new story all prepared – and never a mention of Thérèse, of course – she turns up...

No, that was crazy. I was seeing murder and murderers all over the place. There'd surely be flight records. Or maybe she came by train...? How did she get in and out of the valley with no one seeing her? Did she walk? Did she set the *finca* on fire, then simply walk all the way back?

No, it was all crazy. I was going crazy.

I looked out across the valley. Once again I saw everything around me as a painted landscape overlaid with a cracked veneer. A surging violence lay underneath – violence contained and silenced by neat brushstrokes representing trees, cacti, stones, red earth, the sky, people.

Underneath. The 'deep-down' Anna was always on about. I felt this searing life force, coming from far below, driving men and women to love and to hatred, to desire, to longing and madness. To destruction, even. Anna had *needed* to come to Spain – forced here out of love, out of desperation, out of revenge? Who could tell?

9

Later that afternoon a real wind sprang up – a wind that blew the dust into our faces, tore at the trees, bending them this way and that, and shredded the clouds. We went indoors. In Les Montagnes Blanches we had kept our apartment reasonably tidy, with a place for everything and everything in its place. Here, what we didn't need was shoved into the corners or heaped along the walls. Having swept clear a small area of floor, we'd stuck the brush behind the door and left it. Already, though, the cabin was getting messy and cluttered again, almost by itself. The room was hot, full of dead air.

Anna was standing over by the window. There was a look in her face I had seen before: that morning in Les Montagnes Blanches when she'd picked up the scissors threatening to stab herself. But this time she was no longer angry; she seemed stricken almost...

She said: 'Sometimes it's like I don't feel anything any more.'

'What d'you mean?'

'I mean – I don't feel *anything*.'

That's when I saw something in her hand, something bright and glittery.

'But you'll fix that, my good man. I know you will.'

The wind outside seemed stronger than ever. I glanced past her to the window, half-expecting to see a blur of trees, grass, birds, animals and the entire landscape being whirled round the cabin. In the centre, where we were – door shut, window shut – there was an unreal calm.

'Come here, Jack.'

I didn't move.

She held out a jagged shard of glass. 'This is for you.'

Still I didn't move.

'The difference between life and death is being able to feel something, even pain. Make me feel alive, Jack.' She paused. 'Please.'

I could sense the ground giving way beneath me, as if we were on the edge of a slope that would lead us down into a terrible stillness. Above hurtled the debris of the world I'd known before.

Downwards I went. One step, a second step. Another.

'Don't be afraid, Jack. You'll be giving me life.'

As I moved towards her, the heat in the room felt like nails being driven into my skin, and the wooden floor now seemed to burn under my feet like fire.

'Life? But what about... what about our child?'

'Our child? You really believed I was pregnant?'

It took me several seconds to take in what she meant. No child? Nothing?

Nothing... just Anna?

'What! You're saying you're not...? You bitch!'

'That's right, Jack. Get angry. Get really angry. Let it all out.' She smiled. She was still holding the piece of broken glass, offering it to me.

'You fucking bitch... What the hell's going on? If you're not pregnant, why did you come here?'

'Because... because we belong together, Jack. I know we do. Isn't that a good enough reason?'

I still didn't understand. 'What do you want from me?'

'Don't you get it, Jack? We *belong*. Trust me.'

I backed away. Next thing I knew, she'd placed the glass on the palm of my hand. I could feel its sharpness, like a spike that was all cutting edge.

'I know what I'm doing, Jack. It'll be fine. We'll be fine.'

I backed further away until I was right up against the wall.

'Afraid?'

Before I could reply, she'd taken another step. 'You've hurt women before, I should know. You bastard.'

'That was different.'

'Was it? Come on.'

She was standing right in front of me. I threw the piece of glass on the table, where it landed next to the saucerful of melted candle stubs.

'Afraid – to hurt me?' Then she half-smiled. 'Or afraid you'll like it? Come on.' She was breathing in short gasps. 'Do it for me... so I won't do it to myself... I know you... I know you'll like it... and that's good. Good for us.' There was sweat glistening on her face, and her eyes were drifting in and out of focus.

She went down on her knees, and before I could sidestep her she'd put her arms around my legs and was pressing her face into my groin.

'Come on, you bastard. I can feel you want to, that you'd like to. That you're getting excited.' She began rubbing her face against the front of my jeans. 'Yes, I know you'd like to hurt me. Don't be afraid.'

She'd gripped the outline of my prick between her teeth and was sliding her mouth up and down. Then she drew back.

'Who do you want me to be? Someone you'd like to get back at? Here's your chance: say what you want, call me who you want.'

I was struggling to free myself, but she'd tightened her grip; her face was twisted towards me, a line of spittle running down the side of her mouth. Her eyes seemed focused on something far away.

'Come on, there must be someone you'd have loved to hurt, to make cry out.' She reached up, grabbed my hand and pressed it against her shoulder. 'Dig your fingernails into me. Mark me. Close your eyes if you want. Dig your fingernails in. Claw at me!'

As she dragged my hand down her shoulder I could feel my fingertips starting to grip on to her skin.

Then I let go.

I'd had enough of her crazy stuff – the mind games before, and now this. This was worse. I tried to push her away. If she wanted to fuck, couldn't we just fuck and be done with it?

'What about some bitch that gave you a hard time? Or that you fancied and she wouldn't let you touch her? What about Thérèse? I bet you fancied her – that little slut who got wet at the sight of older men. Remember her, Jack? Up in the mountains? A slut, a little-girl slut. Maybe even fucking her own father, so they told us.' Anna's breath was coming in such short gasps she could hardly speak.

She slid her hand down and began to unzip me.

I had stopped trying to push her away. The two of us fell to the floor.

Afterwards, I lay in her arms while she stroked my hair.

10

A few weeks passed. Two, three – maybe more? Anna and I certainly had no idea. Now and again, first thing in the morning, the air seemed a little chilly – not Scottish chilly, but Scottish warm rather. In the full sun it felt almost as hot as ever. We slept, we wandered, we sat round, we cooked, we ate, then we slept again. There was no mention made of the episode with the piece of glass. For a time we became a couple who at least tried to ease each other's pain. It could have been our very own Happy Ending.

An ending, certainly. No love story, but then perhaps there never had been. Not with Thérèse, Anna or any of the others back to the prodigy days and the happy childhood. So many women, so many stepping stones I've stood on to keep myself safe and dry.

Every day soon became yesterday repeated over. When food had begun running low – Rosa's tinned supplies all but giving out, we lived on fruit, on vegetables and more vegetables – we returned to Toni and Charlie's shack and ransacked it for tins of coffee, packets of rice, lentils and pasta from the food safe, dried milk, biscuits. We picked the veg from the garden, took down the tent and moved everything into what had now become 'our' cabin. We kept ourselves to ourselves, fence-posted safe and secure inside Paradise.

Once the gas canisters were empty, we returned to raid Toni and Charlie's woodpile. Having hacked the shack door free with an axe, we piled it high with timber and carried it back like a stretcher. A couple more stretcher trips kept us going in firewood for cooking. For a while, at least – then it was back for a couple more loads. The pump water was down to a mere trickle. The river was a gully of bleached stones, the rope dangled high above a bathing pool that now was nothing more than a stench of stagnant river mud and weeds.

We'd almost stopped listening to the radio; the signal was getting poorer as the batteries faded. Occasionally we tuned in and again would catch the odd Spanish word that not even we could fail to understand:

Baghdad, bomba, Basra, violencia, terrorismo...

From time to time we *talked*. That is, Anna talked. This was just a holiday, she kept saying, our lazy, do-only-what-we-want-and-only-when-we-want-to holiday before we returned to real life in the real world.

Every so often I took part in these discussions. Sometimes I even tried to exceed my role as her straight man.

'The real world? You mean a house, a job, a kid.'

'And a future, Jack. Stop talking like some clapped-out old hippie. It's not you. You're a doer. You fix things. You need to fix things because...'

And there we were, in familiar territory once again – heading back down the Analytical Road to Nowhere.

Guerra, Iraq, Americanos, muerte...

'Is that the real world you're so keen about?' I said to her one evening after we'd switched off the radio. 'Somewhere where we might get blown up any moment, when we're sitting having an after-dinner drink in our home or in a bar, at the cinema or getting on a bus? Terrorism is— '

' —just an excuse. You could get run down crossing the road.'

That afternoon we had found a bottle of cheap Spanish brandy while making one of our occasional attempts to arrest the disorder in the cabin. After nearly a mugful each we were drunk.

'Not *deliberately* run down. No drivers are *deliberately* trying to kill pedestrians. Out here, there are no drivers at all. Much safer.'

'We're not safe anywhere, Jack. They don't need bombs. A few spores and bacteria in the drinking water...'

'Let's stick to brandy, then. Part of our master plan for survival.'

'I'm serious, Jack. All this talk about smuggling old Soviet radiation or plutonium or whatever it is – it's irrelevant.'

'Won't be irrelevant if it falls on your head.'

'All they need do is fly a plane into a nuclear plant. Into Torness, say, just along the coast. Edinburgh would be toast.'

'That rhymes! And so does...' I summoned up the full concentration of a mugful of *Soberano*, then came out with: 'If you think you need a shrink – then have another drink!'

I poured us each another generous ration. Anna looked on in silence.

'Cheers!' I drank.

'We can't stay here for ever, Jack. Let's leave all this and go.'

'Go?' Too drunk to play the straight man any more, I'd turned into an echo.

'Let's go home.'

That was when the table began rippling under my fingers and the distant stars to flip over, one constellation at a time. I focused on Anna's hand lying on the armrest of her picnic chair, seemingly rising and falling like a small boat at anchor next to me.

'Home?' The word had a familiar sound but seemed to make no sense. 'Home?'

'Our home, Jack. The home that you and I will make together.'

To echo 'together' proved to be completely beyond me. As Anna continued talking, her voice took on a hypnotic *prrr* that grew more soothing, more comforting. My eyes closed.

When I awoke I found myself seated at the table alone. The stars had settled back to normal. Feeling only slightly queasy, I stood up. A drink of water and a pee later, I went indoors.

Anna was deeply asleep, snoring. It was the first time I had heard her snore. I lay down beside her and reached out my hand to give her hair an affectionate ruffle. Seconds later, and without knowing whether or not I had managed to stroke her hair, I too was fast asleep.

11

One morning we climbed the hill opposite to visit Sven's house.

Here and there, through the gaps in the trees, the dark green mass was shot through with fierce sunlight and the white-stone glare from the near-dry river bed. I pointed out some of the sights not yet visited: Dolores's house, the red-dust trail leading to Buena Suerte, the distant mountains. We listened to the breathless rustle, rustle, rustle of the trees. Sven's place gave me the creeps.

No Sven. This time the door stood open. There was no one about.

Before I could stop her, Anna had walked straight in.

'Just for a quick look round. Not like in Les Montagnes Blanches. I don't think there'll be any bottles of Bollinger waiting to be liberated!'

Meaning to get her straight back out again, I followed.

The interior was like a sauna furnished for Spartans, or, more precisely, for the Spartan on his own. There was a single wooden chair, a wooden kitchen table, bare except for a neatly trimmed green mosquito coil mounted on its metal frame ready to be lit, a box of matches at the side. A single bed with a dark blue cover had been made up without a wrinkle. One mug, one plate and one set of fork, knife and spoon were laid out on a shelf. With the shutters half-closed against the heat, there was a familiar atmosphere to the place, like a church.

'What does he do all day?'

'Keeps himself in touch with God, so Toni said. He calls it the Great Oneness. We should leave.'

Not that there was anything to stay for: once you'd had a drink of water, looked at the view and re-catalogued the cutlery, that was about it. Not a book, not a picture, not an ornament even, unless you counted the mosquito coil.

Despite the heat, the room felt chilly; probably just the sweat cooling off. Everything was made of wood, except the cooking area, which was a neatly swept rectangle of firebricks that had a polished metal backplate leading up to the stone chimney. A nest of crisscrossed twigs was set ready to be lit, and a dozen or so logs were stacked on either side. Two large hand-made boxes, like seamen's chests, were the only other furniture. His food in one and his clothes in the other, presumably. Was this true solitude or true loneliness?

Not a church; a monastery more like, or a hermit's cell – every word we spoke seemed to break a vow of silence. I could sense a pitiless masculinity stripped of everything, leaving exposed only spiritual strength or weakness. I wasn't sure which.

We were turning to leave when I nearly collided with a shadow standing in the doorway. 'Sven! I'm sorry. We just came to— '

The shadow looked painfully thin, as if its arms and legs were being invisibly stretched even at that moment. A man perpetually on the rack, by the look of things.

'You are leaving.' This was not a question.

'Yes. Yes, of course.'

He stood aside to let us pass through the door.

Once we were all standing outside again, he seemed to relax.

With great formality, he nodded to each of us, placing his hand on his chest in a truly biblical gesture of greeting.

'I have been gathering herbs.' He laid a canvas sack down beside the door. 'Herbs to heal the body and the spirit.' He wore a bright red NO A LA GUERRA! sweatshirt and jeans. His every word and movement seemed weighted with gravitas.

I introduced Anna.

She tried her social best. 'Nice place you've got, Sven.'

He looked closely into her face. 'You feel at home here?' It was a genuine question. Then the unseen rack was tightened to produce a smile.

He disappeared back inside, returning with two fold-up canvas chairs I'd not noticed before and the single wooden one. They were placed in a small semicircle at the shady side of the cabin, under the rustle, rustle of the trees. Anna and I were invited to sit down. He went inside again, this time coming back with a label-less bottle of clear liquid in one hand and three glasses in the other.

He took the wooden chair and poured us our drinks. We said '*Salud!*' and sipped. The clear liquid, he explained, was a spirit he made from the extra vegetables that he couldn't eat. I believed him. Then followed the usual questions about who, where, when, etc.; he seemed to pay attention to the answers. Unlike Marshall, he had no desire to preach. A church of one, it seemed.

Suddenly I realised he was talking about the fire.

'The door jammed like that...' He nodded to himself. 'It must have been love.'

'What?' He meant hatred, surely? Rosa had jammed the door out of hatred. Or jealousy. Rage.

'Love?' Anna leaned forward. 'But the man who died – Marshall was his name, wasn't it? – was there alone. No?'

'Love. The door was jammed tight on the inside.' Sven took a sip of his firewater. 'Wedged with a metal chisel or something like that. I kicked it out of sight before anyone noticed.'

'The *inside*?' I stared at him: 'If you knew, why didn't you say something?'

'What was there to say? An "accident" was better for everyone. They wanted to die... so they died. It was *their* business.'

From Anna: 'Who's *they*?'

I tried my best to talk through her question. 'You mean – suicide? But – why, Sven? Why would Marshall have wanted to— ?'

'That is how it was.'

'Who's *they*?' Anna repeated, then turned to me: 'You said Marshall was alone.'

'Yes. Marshall was married to Rosa, who— '

Then Sven: 'There was a French girl with him. I never met her – not until it was too late. The two of you came here together, Jack, didn't you? What was her name again?'

I began gabbling. 'Well, Sven, it was a real tragedy. Life, love and death, eh? Anyway, Sven— ' I stood up ' —thanks very much for the drink. Really good stuff, but we'd better get going.'

'*Thérèse*, that was her name. From Paris. I remember now.'

Anna gave me a look of pure hatred. Without a single word to either of us, she got to her feet and strode off down the hill.

I said a quick goodbye to Sven and hurried after her. She marched on, looking neither left nor right. I kept my distance – a good fifty metres behind her, ready to leap for cover if she turned around. She was walking very quickly, and when she came to the shallow ford she didn't even bother removing her trainers, but splashed across as if there was no river there.

Without stopping on the opposite bank to dry off, she continued straight up the slope to the main track, then kept going. I followed. Ten minutes later she took the turn down to Paradise, crossed the building site without a glance, went up the steps and into the cabin.

I stayed where I was at the top of the slope and waited. Sounds of loud banging and crashing came from the cabin. Then silence.

About ten minutes later she emerged carrying the holdall she'd brought when she first arrived. She helped herself to a drink from the water-barrel, then kicked the barrel over. A second kick sent it rolling away in the dirt, spilling water everywhere. Shouldering her bag, she came back up the track. I ducked out of sight into the small wood.

Once on the main track she paused and took a complete look round – a full 360-degree sweep. Was she looking for me? Or else enjoying a last farewell glance round the countryside?

She shouted out, 'You fuckbrained bastard! You can stay here and fucking rot for all I care. You FUCKBRAIN!'

Then she marched off in the direction of Buena Suerte.

12

The cabin had been trashed, near enough. Books, clothes, rice, pasta, tools, torn sacks of vegetables were scattered everywhere. She'd knocked over the small side-table. Having taken the sledgehammer to the shelves, she'd moved on to demolish anything within reach. The sledgehammer had ended up sticking out of the wall, embedded between two splintered planks. I started to pull it out, then stopped. For a moment I stood quite still, my hand resting on the shaft. Through the open door came the only living sound for miles around: the cicadas' grinding rasp. Never varying, never ending.

The cicadas, it seemed, had more purpose in life than I had.

I left the sledgehammer lodged firmly in the smashed wall, half in and half out.

Twenty minutes later I caught sight of Anna up ahead. She

was still striding along. I followed.

When she came to where the river marks the boundary of the property, I hid behind one of the two trees at the ford. She marched straight across as before. The water was hardly even ankle-deep. I waited until she had gone some distance ahead, then began to cross.

Halfway over, I slipped.

She must have heard the splash for she halted, then stood watching me flounder the rest of the way on to dry land. She didn't say one word as I approached her. Her face remained rigid with fury. When I was only a few metres short of her, she turned on her heel and continued walking, double-speed.

Even then I could have given up and gone back to the cabin, given up and let Anna walk out of my life. Let her walk to safety.

I could have, but I didn't. Instead, I scampered after her. I caught up and started frisking around on either side of her like a puppy, looking into her face, into the hatred in her eyes. Trying to get her attention. And all the while babbling, babbling:

'I'm sorry, Anna. I should have told you about Thérèse. But I couldn't. Anna. Anna. Listen to me. I'm sorry. I wanted to tell you... when you turned up I wanted to... but... but... you had come all the way and... and I'm sorry. Please, listen. I... I... What do you want? What can I do? Anna, please. Please. I'm sorry. So sorry...' And on, and on.

And on...

It was mid-afternoon when the first red-tiled roofs of Buena Suerte came into view. Beyond, in the distance, the church and its spire stood revealed in an almost empty reservoir. We came to the dried-up river bed, the skeletal trees, a yellow dog lying asleep on the top step of someone's veranda.

It had been a long walk. My pathetic babbling had long since drizzled to a stop. We were tired, sweaty and filthy, hungry and thirsty. Very thirsty indeed.

Anna spoke her first words. 'We'll drink first, then eat. Then talk.'

Jésus's store seemed the best bet.

It was closed.

The street was deserted. Nothing moved. From behind low garden walls came the cicadas' rasping drone.

I went round the back of Jésus's store. Next moment I almost fell on my knees in gratitude: the owner himself was there, relaxing in the shade, enjoying a beer.

Anna and I were soon seated at a rickety metal table. Beefburgers were being cooked. Beer was on its way.

The beers were opened. Our meal began.

We gorged ourselves. In total silence.

Two beefburgers for her. Two for me.

Afterwards, Anna wiped her mouth on a paper napkin. She folded the napkin in half, folded it in half again, then laid it flat on the table. She crossed her arms.

'You know, Jack, you are a real bastard. You abandoned me. You promised me everything, then ran off. Tell me, were you shagging Thérèse when we were up in the Alps?'

'No.' The voice of a clear conscience. 'No, definitely not.'

'Why should I believe you?'

'It's the truth.'

'Oh, yeah? Well, the truth hardly matters now, does it? You dumped me, then just happened to bump into her up the

Eiffel Tower, did you? – was that how it was?'

So I confessed. Apart from the dismal two days *chez* Pablo and Claudine in the Holiday Village Apartments, I told her everything. Thérèse and her father. Marshall and Thérèse. The fire. Rosa and her bruises.

When I had finished, Anna laid her hand on my arm. 'You men are the real romantics, Jack. The truth is that life is really very simple – it is only people who are complicated. People like Thérèse.' She shook her head. 'Feeling responsible, are you?'

'Well, I feel that— '

'Don't worry. Whatever happened at the fire – it was *her* life. Her decision. Her own business, as Sven said. You just stick with that.'

She leaned across the table. The unexpected tenderness of her kiss felt like a burn mark.

'You know, Jack, we should just leave. Together. The two of us. Now.'

'What?'

'I've brought everything we need...' She reached into her bag and flourished something in the air. I couldn't believe what I was seeing.

'You brought my passport?'

'And your bank card. I know you, Jack. I knew you'd follow me.'

'And if I hadn't?'

She mimed ripping my passport in half.

After a pause I said: 'You mean we up and leave everything, just like that?'

'OK then, I'll leave by myself. I came all the way here – and, fuck you, buster, I can go all the way back.'

I said nothing.

'Is that what you want, Jack? To be left alone? Just you and the mosquitoes and the snakes? To end up like Sven? At least he's got the Great Oneness to keep him happy – what have you got?'

Happiness? My mind went blank.

It was as if everything I could hear and see around me – the hot afternoon, the dusty back yard, the glasses and dishes on the table, the rattle of insects – suddenly seemed as meaningless as the pattern on the back of a playing card, a card that had been abruptly turned face down.

For a split second I was utterly *nowhere*.

Then, all at once, I was back in the moment when she'd placed that shard of broken glass in my hand. Her voice clotted with saliva and desire, she was urging me not to be afraid.

And the next time? When she begged me again to cut her – would I say no? If she got angry, would I try to calm her, would I try to hold her close?

Did we really belong together, as she said? We seemed to. Something held us. Not love, but something more ruthless.

Then the playing card was tumbling over and over: I was helplessly adrift among impressions of the heat-stifled cabin, the crazy violence, the smell of beefbrugers and beer, the stunted cacti, the red tiles, stripped trees, the empty sky.

Before I could speak, the playing card was flipped back: once again the two of us were sitting side by side having lunch outdoors behind Jésus's store.

Happiness, she'd said. The happiness I'd felt when playing the piano – that had been real happiness. It had filled me, brimming over until it fell spilling from my fingertips.

But that, I suddenly realised, had been nearly twenty years ago.

Anna was still looking at me, waiting.

Finally, she placed my passport on the table between us. We both stared down at it. She laid her hand over mine. 'OK, you win. This time, anyway.'

We headed into Jésus's store to stock up on the necessaries – as much as we could carry. Then trudged back to Paradise.

March 2004

1

Days passed, and then weeks...

One night I had just come into the cabin and been about to pull off my T-shirt and jeans when Anna called softly over to me, her voice no more than a whisper. She was lying on our bed, her nakedness bathed in moonlight. She murmured: 'Cut me, cut me and let the darkness out.'

Once again she was holding out a piece of jagged glass.

A double take: and we were back in that land of ice and snow. Once again she was threatening to stab herself with the scissors, once again she was turning the edge of the carving knife against herself. We were like sleepers sharing the same nightmare all over again, sleepers who had ceased struggling to wake.

This time I watched my hand reach for the piece of broken glass, and take it.

She laid her fingers over mine and began guiding me: 'Don't be afraid, Jack. I'll show you.'

At first my hand tensed and went rigid, but she kept whispering encouragement. Her skin was slick with sweat and gleamed wetly in the dirty light.

As her hand closed tighter over mine, I could feel the glass, its jagged sharpness, its edge like a chipped razor.

'Come on, Jack. Please.' She stroked my head and the side of my face. 'Please.' She drew my hand nearer. 'There, just under my breast.'

Her hand traced a line across her chest. 'Kiss it first. After you cut me we'll be able to look at the mark you've made. This will be our first, the one that we'll keep fresh – for *us*. So, kiss me.' And she lay back to let me get close.

When I kissed her, I tasted sourness on her skin – not just the sweat, but something else. Her breathing had become more urgent and louder. 'Kiss me again, then lick... gently.' Her arm round my neck, she was pulling me hard against her. 'Then not so gently.'

I did what she asked while she started to nip my ear lobes, my shoulders, with her teeth – small nips that soon turned into real bites.

'That's what to do, Jack. Harder... Harder.'

She began guiding my hand with the splintered shard to where I'd been kissing her.

Together – slowly, but gradually – we descended further into the terrible place that seemed her only refuge. Then a little further...

As the glass cut into it, I could feel her skin stretch and give. The thinnest thread of blood appeared.

'Yes,' she breathed. 'See, Jack. How pure it is. Yes. It will make me feel good. Really.'

Outside, though it was still night, I sensed the air become so hot the trees were catching fire. All around us in the darkness, unseen slitherings and screechings decided matters of life and death. I could feel the near presence of the wild horses, the lizards, the snakes, the birds of prey in all their raw colours...

She drew her finger along the line of blood, lifted it to her mouth and licked it. Then she held it out to me: 'For you, Jack. To taste and to share.'

I turned away.

'Come on,' she said. 'You've hardly started. Come on, lover, that's nothing.'

Before I could stop her, she'd wrenched my hand against her – and another small wound began to bleed, then another.

'Stop it, Anna.' I got to my feet and threw away the glass. It clattered on to the floor, over by the window. 'Stop. That's enough.'

'Help me, Jack. Don't be afraid.' She got up and took a step towards me. 'Help me.' She was almost pleading. But then, with a sudden movement, she took hold of my hand and began pulling me towards her.

She screamed into my face: 'Come on, you bastard, CUT ME! CUT ME!'

Before I knew what was happening, she'd slapped me hard. Then she pushed, trying to knock me over. She grabbed for my arm and dug her fingers in, raking the skin. 'You must, Jack, you MUST!'

'Stop it, Anna. For Christ's sake, what are you— ?'

She hit me hard in the mouth. I tasted blood. When I raised my hand to feel where she'd punched me, she seized it and bit hard.

'Stop it! For fuck's sake, Anna, you've got to stop before things— '

'Come on, you bastard. See how you like it!' She bit the

back of my hand again.

I tried to grab hold of her, to get her still, but couldn't. My hands slithered over the sweat and blood on her skin.

Then she came right up to me, her face pressing into mine, her breasts and stomach thrusting against me. She pushed as hard as she could. I pushed back to keep my balance.

'You bastard, come on, you fucking bastard!' she spat.

I couldn't keep my footing any longer, and we fell. We began rolling about in the mess on the cabin floor, getting tangled in soiled sheets, in sweat-soaked clothes, ropes, tools and all the other rubbish, getting smeared with dirt and dust, kicking our legs out and tearing to get ourselves free of the mess, knocking over chairs, trampling the cardboard boxes. She kept screaming and biting and scratching, tearing at the T-shirt I was wearing. I kept trying to get on top of her, to get astride her, to pin her down and so bring things to a stop.

Finally she relaxed and seemed to give up. I moved to one side and leaned away from her, with my back to the mattress. It was so hot now in the cabin that we could hardly breathe, and I lay there panting. The sweat ran down my body, making the scratch marks sting. At least she seemed calmer. I turned to her.

'Anna, what was all that about? If you— '

Suddenly she'd rolled over, and in one smooth unbroken movement had got to her feet.

She stood glaring down at me. 'If it's not my turn, then it must be yours. See?' She had recovered the piece of glass. Brandishing it, she came at me. I stood up.

She came closer and closer, slashing at the empty air while I backed away, stumbling in the mess. Had she gone completely crazy? Whenever I tried to grab her she'd jerk her arm free.

Another cut, a slash that ripped the front of my T-shirt wide open, just missing my chest.

'Your turn now, Jack – see what it's like to feel pain. You hurt me. You betrayed me. You always let others feel your pain for you – but not any more.'

I caught hold of her arm and tried to twist the glass out of her hand. My grip kept slipping, and she suddenly seemed to have the strength of ten. This was no longer like the scratching and biting foreplay with Thérèse – screaming full-voice and chasing each other through the woods and open country. Anna had became vicious. Vicious, and quite deadly.

Trapped together in the closed cabin, we went for each other. No holds barred. The small table, a packing case, a cupboard, matches, glasses, bottles, candles, tools went clattering everywhere, dishes were smashed, clothing was torn from the nails where it had been hanging. We slammed into the walls and the door.

Gradually I forced Anna up against the wall, but she wouldn't drop the piece of glass. Without warning she bit me so hard on the shoulder that I cried out in real agony. I took a tighter hold of her wrist, twisted it and kept twisting until she screamed with pain. I wouldn't stop, and she wouldn't give in. How much pain did she need? One by one, I tried to prise her fingers free of the glass.

She was bringing it closer. Right up to the side of my cheek.

Then I let her go – and smashed my fist into the wall right next to her face, meaning to frighten her. Again and again I slammed my fist into it, as hard as I could. Hammering with all my strength as if trying to punch my way through.

Next thing I knew we were both staggering backwards on

to the mattress, and her full weight was on top of me. When we fell, she seemed to slide off to one side and come to rest on the floor. Then to lie completely still.

I got to my feet.

'Anna?'

There was no reply. No movement. Nothing.

'Anna, are you all right?'

2

      I wanted to bend down and check that she was OK. Like when she'd pretended before and, stretched across our dining table in Les Montagnes Blanches, had lain in a pool of spilled red wine. She was no longer moving. No groaning, no sighing. Nothing.

I stood in the centre of the cabin, my heart thudding in my chest, my breath coming in great heaves – and had no idea what to do next. At my feet, lying where she'd fallen, was Anna. In the near darkness, her hair spread like torn shadow across her face, her body was hunched and motionless.

The moonlight seeping in cast a grimy stillness over everything in the cabin. I staggered back against the upended wooden crate we used as a night-table. Beside it, next to the stump of candle in its saucer, lay a half-smoked joint. I found myself lighting it up. It tasted the way her skin and hair would have tasted had we shared it after making love. I took a deep draw and around me the room glowed red: the unpainted walls, bare floorboards, the half-rotted blind, the discarded clothes and all the other rubbish...

And Anna.

I felt I was going to be sick. Another deep draw.

Kicking my way through the mess, I wrenched open the door and stumbled outside.

Without caring where I went, I rushed in every direction, blundering from side to side, stumbling through the darkness, colliding with the unfinished walls, the piles of bricks, cement sacks, breeze blocks.

When I found myself at the boundary fence, I gripped the barbed wire and held on. Pain seared into the palms of my hands; the cool night air seemed to harden against the drying blood and sweat on my body. Around me I could hear the endless rasping of the cicadas, the screeches of night birds. I knew there should be stars above me, a line of trees sloping to the right, the stone-dry river bed straight ahead – but I could picture only Anna as I had last seen her, lying on the floor, bloodied and quite still.

I could feel a scream forcing itself up through me, as if from the very core of the earth. A scream that would have filled the entire valley. But there was no breath left in me to let it come out.

Panting now and gasping like I was going to burst, I began running again.

Then I found myself outside the door of the cabin again. I halted. Go back in?

Now what? Now what?

I was running towards the fence. I was struggling to clamber over it. I was ripping my already ripped clothes, ripping the already torn skin from my hands.

Running again as fast as I could, running from that terrible silence in the cabin: I went stumbling along the bank of the river, scrambling on my hands and knees up the slope, stumbling among cactus plants, scrub and trees. I blundered across wheel ruts, falling down, getting to my feet again. At last I came to the dirt track.

Once more, running and running... as fast as I could, as far as I could... my breath in ragged gasps.

I came to what now remained of Toni and Charlie's shack – the gaping hole where we had hacked away the door, plastic sheeting hung like a tattered banner from the roof, two windows had fallen in. There was broken glass everywhere and I could hear the scuttle of cockroaches. Aimlessly I kept picking up things and putting them down again – a waterproof jacket stiff with grime, a single boot, some rope, a paper sack that might have held dried peas or rice but was now ripped open and empty.

When I stepped outside again, I could tell something had changed. The air felt tense and electric. There was a dampness I hadn't noticed before. Back on the path, I kept going, not running this time as I no longer had the strength. Just putting one foot in front of the other.

I found myself standing in front of the looming shadow of the burned-out farmhouse. Its charred shell. Everything was as before: the gutted building, the broken tiles, the blackened timbers lying where they had been dragged into the yard to burn themselves out.

I crossed to the shaky chimney-breast and fumbled in the dim shadows where the mantelpiece had been... Finally my fingers brushed against Thérèse's necklace and silver pendant. I touched it and held its near weightlessness. A moment's calm.

Thérèse was 'complicated', Anna had hinted. Could it really have been Thérèse herself who had jammed the door?

She'd lost too much in her short life and, all alone, could recover nothing. By themselves, no one can. In that burning room had she finally seen a way to bring her sufferings to their close, to find some kind of lasting peace?

Had I helped push her over the edge?

Like I had now done with Anna? Not with fire this time, but with violence and a fistful of broken glass? But never, never in my entire life had I wanted to hurt anyone...

3

Not caring where I was going any more, I wandered off into the darkness, across the open grass and scrub, sometimes half-running, sometimes walking, tripping over roots in the dark, staggering to my feet again and carrying on. Every so often a few heavy drops of rain fell on to the hard-baked ground, hitting me. I hardly noticed.

Then I was standing outside Dolores's house. Around me were the faint outlines of her garden: the rusted van, the rolls of chicken wire; ahead loomed the front porch. Why had I come here? Because this was the only human habitation for miles? Because I wanted to tell someone what I'd done? To confess?

Moonlight was lying like water on the darkened windows. The wooden stair gave slightly as I stepped up to the door. I halted and listened. Not a sound from inside. My hand was on the latch. It lifted.

I went in.

The shuttered windows spread shallow light unevenly across the room, greyness and darkness leaking weakly into each other. Side by side in the middle of the floor, the only clear area in the room, Dolores's mattress and baby Miguel's drawer were anchored among the sea-drift of clothes and toys. Mother and son were fast asleep. Carefully I crossed over to them, testing the boards in case they creaked. Dolores's hair had unravelled over her pillow, spilling darkness over the paler patchwork cover of her bed. A cloud must have passed in front of the moon at that moment for, in one unbroken sweep, the room was abruptly erased all around me.

I knelt down. I was about to touch her lightly on the shoulder, to wake her.

My hand was only centimetres above her sleeping head...

'Don't move.'

The voice came to me out of the darkness over by the window. A light shone into my face, blinding me. The next instant, Dolores had rolled free from under my hand and was standing up. I began getting to my feet.

'Stay there.'

I remained on my knees at the side of the mattress, looking away from the brightness, down at the pillow and the indentation made by Dolores's head. 'I'm sorry, I— '

'Do not speak.' Sven was standing over me.

Behind me I could hear Dolores picking Miguel up out of his drawer.

There was a thud like a muffled gunshot above me, then a second, a third, then a thousand. Rain, heavy rain falling full-force, hammering on the roof...

Or was it really rain? It was thudding so loudly and so close as to be almost inside me; blood roared in my ears. A dizziness I couldn't shake myself clear of.

Sven grabbed my arm and twisted it. I heard myself scream.

There was a sudden clatter: something dropped from my hand on to the floor. I looked down and could just make out the piece of jagged glass lying at my feet. I must have been holding it ever since I'd rushed out of the cabin and started blundering about in the darkness. Even when climbing the slope, I must have been still clutching it in my hand. Right up to the moment when I'd leaned over Dolores's face.

I hadn't meant her any harm, I wanted to tell them, but I couldn't seem to make the words come out.

Like a curtain being opened just then, the cloud passed and I saw the two of them staring at me. Four slats of shuttered moonlight measured the distance between us. Miguel, cradled in Dolores's arms, had woken up and begun crying. Dolores soothed him.

Again I tried to rise. 'Please—'

'Don't move.'

I struggled to get to my feet, but couldn't. I stayed as I was, half-kneeling, half-crouching.

'What do you want?' Sven asked.

'I... I was...' I began, not knowing how to go on.

Meanwhile, Dolores had picked up the piece of glass from the floor. She was looking at it. 'You want give me *this*?'

I could see its sharpness glitter as she turned it over.

'From your girlfriend, yes? From Thérèse? Something to remember her?' she continued, then turned to Sven. 'He is no danger.'

Another wave of dizziness hit me. The piece of broken glass – from *Thérèse*? I wanted to say, *Anna gave me it*. Why did they think that Thérèse had...?

I needed to sit down, but there was nothing within reach except for Dolores's mattress. My mouth had gone so dry I could hardly speak, even if I'd known what to say.

She was holding out her hand towards me. '*Gracias* – but it is for you.' She paused. 'It is better. No?'

She was thanking me for a piece of jagged glass? What the fuck was going on? I looked from one to the other. Were they both mad? Uncontrollably I started to shake and shiver all over, as if I was freezing, despite the sweat running down my back.

Above me the rain hammered so loudly I could hardly hear what was being said. Turning from one to the other, I shouted: 'What? What did you say?'

Then I realised that Dolores wasn't holding out a piece of broken glass – but Thérèse's silver pendant. I must have been clutching it in my hand ever since leaving the burned-out farmhouse.

Without another word, I grabbed the pendant and ran out of the door.

The rain was lashing down. I stamped my way through the muddy garbage-garden, tripping over tin cans, plastic sheeting, old sacking and bits of wood.

Drenched to the skin, I came to a halt at the gate. I gripped the pendant in my fist, then hurled it as far as I could into the darkness.

4

By the time I'd stumbled through the driving rain, half-slithering and sliding my muddy descent back to Paradise, I was soaked through and utterly exhausted. I returned here at last and slumped down on to the steps of our cabin, too terrified to go inside.

That was several hours ago.

The rain's continued to thunder against the tin roof, every so often a gust of wind sends it cascading over the cabin steps, drenching me. I've not moved out of the way. I've not moved at all. Hardly a muscle even. For me, it is still the moment immediately after Anna slid backwards on to the floor and lay still...

Sitting here, I've hardly been able to stop crying... Or to stop remembering: Les Montagnes Blanches, the Gare du Nord, Thérèse in her dismal Paris flat, her parents in Spain, coming here to the wilderness. Even the earlier years have returned full-force – my parents' unconditional love, their pride and joy in my talent, and, most of all perhaps, my overwhelming relief at being able to slam down the piano lid for the last time. A fine pianist, but not a *very* fine one.

All my life: I've put one foot in front of the other as if there's been nothing to stand on but this imaginary road – solid ground only when it criss-crossed someone else's, especially a woman's. Every step of the way has seemed the next step, the only step. So effortless, and so inevitable... Is this how the damned recognise each other? By whatever's driving them mercilessly onwards? By the ease with which they can explain away everything – even to themselves? By the curses they repeat as if they were words of encouragement, words of forgiveness? Desire, and exhaustion. Beyond, there is always pain. For those trapped in hell, pain offers a kind of release.

Saying Anna's name over and over…Wanting her… Steeling myself to go back into the cabin… Telling myself I *must*… Picturing the scene inside…

If not love, there had been a sort of truce between us. Even hell, it seems, has its familiar corners where the damned can find rest…

There's a painful grinding of metal on metal as the door's unoiled hinges turn. I enter the cabin on tiptoe.

Despite the filthy window, dawn has already begun separating into shadow and half-shadow; its early- morning greyness is run through by violence: smashed furniture, torn and trampled clothes. And Anna, in the centre of it all, lying perfectly motionless.

Without meaning to, I take another step towards her… and then another.

Leaning down… gazing at her uncovered body, the crisscross of tattered red lines on her skin trapping the first light of day.

I can still feel the pressure of her fingers as she guided my hand *there*, making a bluish-red slash beneath her breast, and *there*, on the inside of her thigh.

My fingers brushing against the strands of her hair…

For an instant her breasts seem to rise and fall, but very, very slightly. Then there's nothing, no sign of her breathing. No sign of…

Then there is. The very slightest, the very faintest...

Or is there?

I step quickly back. I should look for my passport. Grab some money. Some clothes.

But if I leave her like this, she'll be found. Not for days, maybe, not even weeks, but someone will come and discover... whatever's left.

Someone will be sure to come. Sven, Dolores, Rosa, someone. They'll call out. They'll rap on the door. They'll push it open. They'll find her lying there, and they'll *know*. How long until they come? And by then... Poor, poor Anna, even if I cover her. By then she'll be...

She's looking at me. Her eyes are open, and she's *looking* at me. A scream sticks in my throat. Everything is possible now. The dead are among us...

'Jack?'

As if she's coming awake.

Now she's half-sitting up. Now she's leaning across to me, her hand reaching up to smooth my dripping hair, lightly stroking the side of my face. Her living voice, the touch of her hand.

Exhausted to my very heart and bones, I ease myself – sodden clothes and all – down onto the floor beside her.

She carries on half-whispering my name and saying again how she knew I would come back. How certain she is that we belong together. How sorry she is for trying to make me do something I wasn't ready for. Sorry for pretending. How tired I must be, she says. If I like, she will undress me, and then we can lie on the bed in each other's arms, holding each other. Comforting each other.

5

A sudden scrabbling of wings and claws on the tin roof just above the bed has awoken me.

There's still a dampness in the air, a chill almost. Outside, the meaningless cicada noise sounds muffled. As usual, insects buzz and hit against the dirty window, then fly off.

I sit up in bed, kneeling on the mattress to look out of the window, expecting to see the same unfinished buildings, the same dried ground, the same bushes and trees... Since the beginnings of time itself, almost every single day out here in the wilderness must have begun like this: the heat, the insects, the sun, the parched red earth. It is the world we live in.

But today looks different. Very different. Drawn up from the sodden ground round our cabin, a thick mist has all but blotted out the valley. There are hardly any trees to be seen any more, no bushes or scrub, no river. After the first few metres, the red-earth track leading out of Paradise blurs to nothing. Just like those mornings back in Edinburgh when the whole city – the solid sandstone tenements, the tarmac, the cobbles and pavements – was turned into ghost houses and ghost streets by *haar*, a sea fog so dense that the castle itself disappeared. Here, in the wilderness, it seems now that the whole world has been erased.

Not really, of course. For soon enough, when the haze has dissolved, the sun will begin scorching the valley once more: the yellowed grass will take on the beginnings of colour, the trees will turn to a tinder-brittleness ready to flame at a touch, the stones will burn without fire. The sky will become a fierceness no one dares look into.

*

I have just switched off the little radio. Even with my poor Spanish I could understand the words that really mattered:

Madrid, muerte, dos cien, bomba, estación, tren, explosión, horror, carnicería, pasajeros, bomba, bomba, muerte...

Madrid. Only a few hundred kilometres away.

Outside, I can see Anna sitting at the table; the Martini umbrella hangs sodden and bedraggled. For once it's not been unfurled. After our fight last night she'd pretended to be dead. Like she'd pretended back in the Alps. Soon our life together will return to the way it was before – how can I find the energy to stop it? Since leaving home all those years ago, I've done my best to blame the past, and succeeded. That way I've given myself an alibi for life. The trouble is, *that's* all I've ever had. Not a life, merely an alibi for one.

Anna's having breakfast. In front of her there's a mug of coffee with its protective saucer, a dish of berries, some biscuits. When I appear at the door, she will offer me coffee, something to eat, and it will be yesterday all over again...

She has tucked a coil of loose hair behind her ear and leans towards me.

'I felt close to you last night, Jack. Really close.' Then she touches me on the arm. 'I know you didn't want to... not like I did. But it's the start of something, isn't it? Our new beginning.'

I nod like I'm agreeing. I want to tell her about Madrid, about the terrible bombing, the killing of two hundred innocent commuters. This is the world we live in now, I want to say to her – a world where we are no longer innocent. Innocence no longer has any meaning, nor has guilt.

'We had a fight, Jack, but we've made up. Couples do that.'

A couple – is that what we are? A country-loving couple in the safety of their country retreat? A couple living their days and nights, making their plans?

Around us as we finish breakfast, the sun's glare has already burned off the morning mist. The countryside's whitening to its usual almost invisibility of haze, the heat holding the trees, the scrub and the air itself in its exhausted grip. I sit back, ready to let the day flow into me.

Anna suggests we go for a walk. The track leading out of Paradise seems like a river flooded by light. Briefly, there's a sense that we are about to be swept away in a rush of glittering brightness.

As we climb the slope to the main dirt road, I happen to look up and catch sight of a solitary bird set like a full stop in the otherwise unmarked blue sky. Whatever's been written up there, before it or after, has faded to nothing. The bird hangs motionless, poised on invisible currents, utterly still, utterly alone. For a moment I imagine the wilderness as the bird must see it, far below: dust-red earth and dried-out trees, an empty landscape criss-crossed by empty paths and tracks. The two of us trailing a cloud of red dust.

We continue walking. I glance at Anna, intending to point out the bird which I think might be an eagle. Instead, I find myself touching her on the arm.

She's smiled back.

I leave my hand resting where I've placed it. A comforting feeling, perhaps even for both of us.

When I next look, the eagle has vanished from sight as if it had never been. We stop for a moment. There, spread out below us, is all that remains of Paradise: its sketch-plan of familiar grey and black outlines, the breeze-block squares and breeze-block rectangles of uncompleted buildings. Everything looks smudged in the heat. The stretch of river – for today, at least, thanks to the heavy rain – is an onward flow of reflected blue sky, trees and sunlight with scatterings of shade and coolness.

I slip my arm round Anna's waist. We continue walking. The day burns hotter at every step we take.